About the Author

Patrick Church has worked in cinema from the '60s through to the present day. His passion for it shines through in *The Smallest Show on Earth,* this engaging autobiography. Spending most of his career as a projectionist Patrick shows how he guided cinema through the competitive advent of TV and continues on in a Picturehouse in Bury St Edmunds.

Welcome to my world

For my wife, Geraldine,
Who supported me through
thick and thin…

Patrick Church

THE SMALLEST SHOW ON EARTH

AN AUTOBIOGRAPHY

A CIP catalogue record for this title is available from the British Library.

ISBN 9781786297990 (Paperback)
ISBN 9781786298003 (Hardback)
ISBN 9781786298010 (E-Book)

www.austinmacauley.com

First Published (2017)
Austin Macauley Publishers Ltd.
25 Canada Square
Canary Wharf
London
E14 5LQ

Acknowledgments

I thank my uncle John whom without his encouragement,
I would never have got started in this crazy world of Film Exhibition.

To all my friends and colleagues along the way who have succumbed to
my whims and needs
to get it right; I thank them all for being my helping hands.

FOREWORD

I started thinking about putting my life down in writing several years ago; to tell the story of myself and explain the reasons for this burning drive that has always lain within.

Perhaps my wife and son can understand that I can't help the way I am and I love them both to bits, but not being a very academic person I had to work twice as long as everyone else to keep on top.

CHAPTER 1

March 1947 – winter had arrived late that year and down a narrow suburban street of Peterborough in a small terraced house was my mother, heavily pregnant and alone with an 18-month-old baby asleep in the next room. My father, who was nearing the end of his National Service would have to be away, but the baby wasn't due for another three weeks and he would be on leave then.

But as the pacing of the floor became more strenuous and the feeling of "something's going to happen" took over all other reasoning she checked the baby asleep in the next room. He was warm, fed and content and would hopefully sleep throughout the night. It was now gone eleven o'clock. A peep through the curtains showed a clear frosty night, the stars shining out brightly above the snow covered rooftops. Glancing down, the snow had been piled onto the edge of the pavement making it look at least four feet deep. From the light of the two dimly lit street lamps, she could see there was not a soul about, still, if needs be it would be easy to get help from her friends. They were only two doors away, she thought to herself. The pains suddenly started again this time more urgent than before, with a coat wrapped around to keep out the biting cold, it was time to summon help.

Once out on the street the sudden blast of icy cold air seemed to numb out all other feelings as she slowly made her way through the hard packed snow. Only two doors away but it could have been a mile. At last she made it. She reached out and knocked on the door as she was struck by another sudden burst of pain. As the door opened and the light spilled across the pavement, there was my mother, crumpled on the ground in a mound of snow with a newborn baby, yes! I had arrived, my life was about to begin.

Peterborough! My father's birthplace; and here resided all his many family members some of whom I grew to know well in later years. Granny and grandad lived a few streets away although I don't remember them until much later in my life.

Me, out and about 'dig that hat'

Me and big brother Pete

My earliest recollection of childhood is riding on a bus in Peterborough. I must have been about three years old and my mother worked as an usherette at the Odeon cinema (even at that age I had an unknown connection) and we would be riding into the city to meet her. Soon after that we all moved to live in a small village cottage at Elston near Newark, Nottinghamshire.

Dad, standing on the 'top road' waiting for a bus

This was my mother's home which had now become available as my other Grandad had died and granny Edgeling had moved into a home. It was decided this would be a good move as dad had elected to stay in the army as a regular, and mum would be back on her home ground. So, here my elder brother and I flourished in the country life with a large garden to play in surrounded with fields. Summer months of haymaking were our most favourite times, as we always got to help the local farmer Mr Hickson. What a joy! I can see him now, hitching us up on the top of the hay wagon where we would ride down the village to his farmyard, then run all the way back home unhindered and wait for the next day so as to do it all over again.

Riding on the Hay wagon

Having fun with farmer Hickson

Dad and his two boys

(Life in the country, happy days)

School life soon followed.

The next event that I still vividly remember was being taken for a car ride with a smart uniformed lady, my brother sitting beside me. She told us "you're going to be looked after whilst mummy's in hospital, at an orphan school."

What a strange time this turned out to be, from being carefree and happy, to be thrust into this regimented way of life. I'm sure now that it was a very nice place, just so different and it's the different things that stay in the memory, like a bedroom with about twenty beds all lined up in two rows. Waiting in line each morning for a spoonful of cod liver oil followed by a sweetie if you didn't spit it out. How difficult it was starting a new school again.

After what seemed like an eternity our father arrived to take us back home, he said "Mummy is waiting at home and you have a baby sister!"

A WHAT???

Learning to look after sister Susan

Dad had been discharged from the Army due to his failing eyesight and had had several different jobs since coming home. Sometimes we noticed he was at home for more time than others.

The next two years were taken up with all the boyish pranks. We each had our own private hiding places and probably got up to more mischief than we should have done, and of course there was looking after sister. So many times we took her in her pram to the top of the hill, only to then let go of the pram and watch it roll down the other side. On most occasions my sister would be tipped out half way down. Good fun, but we eventually got caught.

This became my 'Dan Dare' era where, as long as we were good and stayed quiet through Radio Newsreel, we could listen to Dan Dare before bed. With my imagination in overdrive, he was my hero of the day. I even fashioned a pilot seat out of the apple tree bough as it had this chink in it, and you would often find me on a Dan Dare imaginary mission.

My famous pilot seat was in this tree

A trip to town was a bus ride into Newark always a big event and this was to be the day for it. After the usual shopping, all of us looking wide eyed at all the things we couldn't have, my father announced "we are going to the pictures!"

After a barrage of questions all we got was "wait and see" and see I did!!!! I drank every moment of it in. The brightly lit sign SAVOY, the round glass box office in the middle of the foyer. Then, once inside this sea of empty seats and what seemed like a giant curtain with coloured lights, I was completely mesmerised with it all! When that curtain started to open and this new magical experience unfolded before me I was hooked!

They Called them
"CANOE COMMANDOS"

Jose Ferrer, Trevor Howard

COCKLESHELL HEROES

For weeks and weeks afterwards I drove everyone mad re-enacting 'The Cockleshell Heroes' and our usual weekly session of Dan Dare on the radio would never be the same again.

It was during one of these moments that I had hoodwinked my brother to playing out a scene with me. We were parachutists jumping out of the airplane, alright it was only off the roof of the old pig sty, but, as you jumped, you had to yell "Airborne"!!!

This was great. I could see all the scenes of the film in my mind but someone always spoils the moment. It was my brother who came crashing down and split his lip open by bashing his knee under the chin, teeth straight through! He ended up in hospital for stitches. If only he had shouted "airborne" and got into the part it might not have happened!

All togged up in our Sunday best

My only memories of the next year was the day I was asked if I would like to see my baby sister who had been 'still born'! I obviously couldn't understand the enormity of this only to be taken upstairs and seeing the large dresser drawer open to reveal this doll-like image. "This is your sister, Wendy," my mother said to me. Only many years later was the significance of the moment fully realised.

On a lighter note there was my dad who had purchased from a mail order catalogue a two-stroke engine that would fit onto a push bike and turn it into a moped, the hilarity we all had at him pushing this contraption fixed onto the back of his cycle, jumping on then phut! phut! cough. He never did get it going and finally sold it on to someone else.

At the end of the village road just before turning onto the top road there was this very large palatial looking house at the front it had a race course (for pony and trap racing) all measured out with white stakes. The entire place was shielded with woodland. At the rear, via another driveway, there were several out houses which apparently were used for breeding maggots. At our age – what was a maggot farm? We just knew that if the wind was in the wrong direction people would say Curly Myers is stirring his stock again. I remember him as a larger than life character who always wore a large Stetson and drove around in this open-topped

American Cadillac. He also had the biggest Great Dane dog I have ever seen. When it went walk-about around the village people would run indoors, but I loved him and would hang on his neck and be carried down the road. What a softie he was until one night. Our own dog was on heat and locked in the wash house for her own good. He must have got the scent and came a calling. All I remember is this terrible fracas going on in the early hours of the morning and there he was baying in our garden. Then with a wild lunge, a crash and a bang he knocked the wash house door clean off its hinges. All good fun!

There was the day that the maggot farm caught fire, a big event for us. My elder brother and I raced across the fields to see the action, but when we got there, my goodness, what a stench! The ditches all around were flooded with water and all this rotting meat and maggots was floating past.

It was too good an opportunity to pass up. He had to go in, so, older brother, in you went and boy was you in a mess! You scrambled out and raced off home! When I finally got there you were standing in the middle of the garden being hosed down before being let into the house. Now was that fun or what? And all those white stakes they had marking out the race course, well half of them ended up in our wash house as firewood.

CHAPTER 2

Rebels at large!

My next big event was another visit to the cinema, but this time it was more memorable than ever. It was just me and Dad, a birthday treat! I felt ten feet tall stepping on that bus and waving my brother, sister and mother goodbye. To this day I shall never forget just what Richard Todd as Rob Roy did to me and a whole load of new adventures lay ahead.

Richard Todd as

Rob Roy

The Highland Rogue

It was also at that time Dan dare had been taken over by BIGGLES, so different adventures were to be had from my apple tree pilot seat.

Thereafter life seemed to take a downhill slide, or maybe I was now old enough to notice the changes; Dad was home all the time, out of work. There was another baby on the way and my brother and me always seemed to be in trouble for one thing or another. At night though, head under the blankets, I could always be Rob Roy, Dan dare or Biggles. Soon after, another brother came on the scene so we had to look after sister more than we wanted to.

Our cottage was quite small for all of us. Just one living room with a large black-leaded range, oven one side and hot water boiler the other. A low beam ran across the middle and there was a walk-in larder with our only sink and a cold-water tap. When you opened the door at the back of the room, there were the stairs which took you up and directly into the bedroom. The door ahead led into another bedroom and that was the entire cottage interior, one living room and two upstairs rooms, but outside led to a spacious wash house with a coal-fired boiler in one corner. This was used for the regular Monday washday and to fill the tin bath on bath days. This room also served as a playroom on rainy days, but not Mondays. Every Monday we watched and tried to help mother keep the boiler going and have a go with the 'dolly pegs'. These were bigger than us, a wooden centre shaft with four feet and a cross bar handle which was worked left and right to agitate the dirty clothes in the tub. As for the mangle for ringing out the water from the clothes me and my brother had turns in feeding in the dripping clothes or turning the handle to make the rollers go round, not forgetting to move your hands or they too would go through, what fun.

Next to the wash house was the lavatory and as you opened the door this large wooden seat with a massive hole seemed to beckon you in, and oh yes 'that bucket'! We helped dad on many occasions to dig a hole to put the contents in. The garden covered a large area flanked on two sides with a dyke that ran down the side under the road and away. This was often full of fast flowing foaming water draining off the fields during the rainy seasons. A pig sty was half way up the garden, which was now used to house our chickens. My Biggles seat apple tree was just outside the wash house door and there was another larger one at the bottom of the garden, beside a plum tree. This was our domain and playground.

Although being surrounded by fields we often ventured further. Elston was a small village off the A46 locally called 'the top road' between Newark and Nottingham. You could drive into the village. Ours was the first habitat about half a mile from the top road and if you just followed the road round, past the schoolhouse and church you came back onto the A46 about a mile further up. This was often a round trip when walking the younger ones.

It was during one of these walks that I had an experience that still haunts me to this day, I was walking my little sister and pushing baby brother in a pushchair just a normal sunny round the block walk when one of those shooting brake style cars with the woodwork round the windows slowed up and stopped a little further down the road. Everything was still and quiet and there was no other traffic or people to be seen. Then a man and woman got out of this motor and started slowly coming towards me. I have no idea why but a fear swept through me like nothing I had ever experienced before I placed my sister on the foot rest of the push chair turned and ran like the wind, in total fear of what, I will never know. However in my later years looking back I often wonder if it could have been Ian Brady & Myra Hindley who were abducting children from that area around this time

Life at home seemed to have become strained over the year that had just passed. I remember over hearing my mother say, "When poverty comes in the door love goes out the window," words that etched into my brain even though they were not meant for my ears. My elder brother and I seemed to go into a rebellious stage around this time, with school being an optimum choice to rebel against.

Ours was a typical village school one very large classroom divided between two teachers and a smaller room for the infants. The main classroom had a large open coal fire with the headmistress's desk just to the side of it. That was Mrs Wright, or Polly Wright as we used to call her, no idea why, you just did!

She was a real school madam, severe and strict and loved to make an example of anyone miss behaving in front of the entire class. It used to be a whack with a broad leather belt brought out with great ceremony from the back of her cupboard. My brother and I were often recipients of this little ritual and never were very endeared to her, especially on the summer days when she would strike fear in your heart by saying "I think we will take the piano outside and have some dancing". A row of eldest boys all tugging and pushing that blasted piano through those double doors into the playground, then it would start. "Come on you boys, heel, heel, toe" while she banged out 'The Bluebell Polka'. We gave it heel, heel, toe alright. As I previously said we had become rebels, and after a strained day at school decided to get even. Polly Wright drove a car a gold coloured Ford popular, so in our eyes that made her posh. We had this idea to lay some old tree branches across the road so she couldn't go home, then hidden away watched for the fun. "Here she comes," my brother said just as the car screeched to a halt. The door flew open and out she shot, strutting up and down, but no one was in sight. All we could see was our bits of branch flying over the hedgerows. Nice One!

We played this game several times after that until the inevitable happened. Yep, caught red handed, well, my brother was. I dived in a roadside ditch and never got noticed. Next morning in school the lecture began as the cupboard opened and the belt was ceremoniously paraded. I did have a little pang of guilt that my brother was taking all the flack but he was the oldest. Whilst he was being thrashed he kept blurting out "He was there," "He was there." We kept our heads down for a while after that, but not for long. It must have been those summer days that did it as we decided no school for us, we would play in the woods all day So that's what we did for a whole week, just bumming around having fun. We had it off to such a fine art that we could be home at dinner time and back across the fields before anyone noticed us. We used to get away early by telling mother we were playing cricket and it was my turn to bat, bowl, etc. What fun we had that week fooling everybody, but on creeping home on the Friday afternoon, who was at our house, oh no, Polly Wright, giving it all that superior headmistress stuff and ranting on that no one had ever played truant on her before. So in front of our gob smacked parents and her we had to come clean and explain how we had spent the week. We so expected a good leathering but after Polly's departure our parents just melted with laughter and we got away with it.

Life had settled into a rut. Dad was still out of work and we seemed to become more self-sufficient than ever. 'Wooding', that was the time when every field had a hedgerow and we would be dragging an old pram round and fill it up with old dead pieces of wood found in readiness under the hedgerows. This wood would be stacked in the wash-house, then used to supplement the dwindling coal stock that fed the fire range. We would be outside in all weathers sieving the ashes to find any cinders that could be re-burnt. During the summer months we would be out picking blackberries and any other fruit that came to hand, mostly scrumped from someone's orchard. Those were the days when homemade tarts and jams were of the norm.

Although some days at home were very tense and strained, we soon learnt when to keep out of the way and the three of us banded together as a unit.

A year passed us by. Dad was still unemployed and we had learnt how to become very self-sufficient or was it just plain survival? The Autumn / winter of 1955 was in its early stages with the dark nights upon us. Every now and again my elder brother and me would accompany Dad on one of our many moonlight raids across the fields. Sometimes it would be to a potato grave, that's where they mound up the harvested potato crop in a long row of about thirty feet standing some eight feet tall, covered in a layer of straw then clad with soil. We would cut a hole in the side just big enough to get your arm in until you could reach the potatoes. We'd fill the bags then carefully replace the straw and dirt and be on our merry way. We had many of these night time adventures, crawling between rows and rows of brussel sprouts careful not to damage any and just take half a dozen off every third or fourth stalk. There were fields of cabbages, cauliflowers, onions oh the list was endless, this was family survival at its finest.

During the dark autumn evenings we as a family unit would be making artificial flowers out of coloured crepe paper Gladiolas was the speciality. During the daytime my brother and me would be scouring the hedgerows and bushes for nice straight sticks of about three feet lengths. These would then be glued and covered in green paper with leaves and coloured petals added to make gladioli.

We would spend the weekends door to door selling these in other villages along the 'top road' towards Newark. On the odd occasion, we travelled into town by bus. Along this route we would be picking out the windows that had our flowers on display.

It was during this period that I got my next cinema visit. I don't remember much of the detail on this visit, only that it was Virginia McKenna and Peter Finch in 'Carve Her Name With Pride'.

Virginia McKenna: Paul Scofield

CARVE HER NAME WITH PRIDE

A few weeks later another visit this time it was Tony Curtis in 'The Black Shield of Falworth'.

Tony Curtis, Janet Leigh

THE BLACK SHIELD OF FALWORTH

That was more like it, a story to fantasise about. This flower selling lark was turning out to be very worthwhile!

It was also during this period that there was talk of us all emigrating to Australia. This was actively encouraged by the governments during this period as they needed an input to help colonise the commonwealth countries of Australia and New Zealand, but alas we were one too many. Three children was the maximum and here we were, now four of us since the birth of Alan our new baby brother. Who knows where we would be today if this had happened?

So life plodded on for us all then out of the blue we were all told that we were leaving Elston to start a new life in a place called Ramsey. This could have been the other side of the world for all we knew, but it seemed that Dad, who had been away for some time now, had secured a job on a pig farm and with it was a large house. It all sounded ideal and caused lots of excitement. The down-side was that we would be moving straight away, by that I mean the next morning, so we only had one night to pack up and get ready (is this what was meant by a moonlight flit?)

Our dad was travelling back home as we prepared so as to be with us by the time the removal van arrived. We were all rushing around doing our bit when suddenly Rosemary Clooney burst forth on the radio with that immortal song 'this old house', so there we all were having a farewell singalong.

As if right on cue early in the morning the door opened and in walked dad only to be faced with a barrage of questions from all us excited kids. In due course the removal van turned up and all our house contents were placed on board. At the very back of all our belongings they placed the settee and chairs and we all climbed in the back. It was one of those removal vans with a high tailboard and canvas curtain top which we had slightly open so we could see out. As we drove off through the village we passed of all people 'Polly Wright' with a group of children on what could only be described as a country ramble. We were quite sure she was out looking for us expecting to find us playing truant again. We waved and shouted from the back of the van. I will never know if she cottoned on as to what was happening, but that was my last recollection of Elston, Polly Wright fading into the distance....

CHAPTER 3

This was the start of what can only be described as a new adventure, as the removal van with all of us and the dog (who had just had puppies) and our worldly belongings made a pit stop at Peterborough. With wide-open eyes we peered out of the back of the van overwhelmed by the sheer size of it all. It was like being in a different world than where we had just come from. We had pulled into a parking area next to the bus station for an hour's stop. The back was opened and out we got for our first look around. Little did I know just how familiar this area would become in later years, but for now it was a walk by the river embankment to exercise the dog, and all of us. I can vividly remember the noise from all the traffic, and so many big red Double Decker buses of which I had only ever seen before in pictures. After an hour's recreation we all piled back into the removal van and set off for the final stage of our journey. After a short while the built up areas we had been staring at in astonishment became fields and hedgerows and we slowly progressed along some narrow winding roads way out into this new open space. Then, without warning, the van suddenly lurched off the road onto this rugged potholed dirt-track. After a short while of being jostled around and all being told to sit down or we would end up getting hurt, the van came to a sudden halt. The driver and his mate came to the rear of the van and lowered the tailboard and out we all tumbled. Standing in a group outside the van we just stood there looking at this great big house in front of us. It had this garden that went all round one side of it with a pathway to the back door. It was time to explore. The house, a double fronted two tenant farm workers house was surrounded with a privet hedge. This separated the two front entrances. The path went around the side of the property and found the back door. The garden spread out along the side and rear of the house. The view from here was so very different from what we had just come from. There were very few trees and a flat landscape so you could see across the fields for what seemed like miles. "Let's have a look inside," and through the back door, we walked into a very spacious kitchen with a large black-leaded range on one wall. We just kept on opening doors and peering in rooms that seemed never ending a walk-in pantry, store rooms, then through another door a toilet! Inside!!! Pull a chain and water came out. It was a long way from going up the yard to that draughty old room with a large wooden seat and a bucket. Across the kitchen, through yet another door and you were in the front hall. The front door was open and our furniture and belongings were being carried in. A quick look in the front room and this was massive! We got shooed out and told to keep out of the way, so upstairs we went. The stairs went straight up onto a landing and, yes more doors. Four bedrooms all of different shapes and sizes, but what was this door that was closed? Better have a look, and what a sight. A small room in comparison to all the others we had looked in, but it had this big white bath and another toilet. WOW!!! No more tin bath in front of the fire and peeing in the pot.

By the time we had completed our exploration the removal van had been emptied of our belongings, which seemed to look rather little in this great big house. During a makeshift dinner we all got to find out that this house was part of our dad's new job which was working on a pig farm further up the track. We would be starting a new school in the town after the weekend, tomorrow we would go into town and do some shopping, but for now everyone up the wooden hill to bed. No one put up any argument against that suggestion. We were all whacked and it looked like tomorrow would be another day filled with excitement.

The morning seemed to come before we had time for any sleep, but that was just us waking up extra early. Looking out of the bedroom window at a clear sunny view of field after field broken by a few hedgerows and the distant houses dotted around on the horizon. It was 'up an' at 'em'. Out in the garden we met the new neighbours. He was also a worker at the pig farm. They had two children of around our own age – that could be handy! After all the usual first meet niceties it was time to get ready for our first venture into the town of Ramsey. No buses, no transport of our own, so it was going to be the first of many long walks to town. After what seemed like a never-ending trek we eventually came round a bend and into view were rows of houses each side and a pavement to walk on. A little further on we saw a sign that read 'Ramsey, an historical fenland town'. "We must be here," I said to the others. As we drew to the end of this road we noticed a high stone wall that seemed to tower above us, then this gave way to an open green with a gateway that read Abbey Grammar School. Though we couldn't have known it then, many years later my sister Susan would be going to that very school.

Just off the green was the Church flanked by Oak and Ash trees. All these things were being taken in as landmarks for finding the way back home because this is where the road turned onto the High Street. As we stood and looked down this street we were amazed at the rows of shops each side. This was a far cry from our one shop village. So down the high street we walked, window shopping with mum and dad, What a drag! About half way down another road joined the street. Great Whyte. As we turned into this we noticed the shops seemed larger and the road opened out into two with a walkway up the middle where a large ornate clock stood overlooking the bus shelter, so this was the main street. We walked up the middle viewing both sides, then just past the bus shelter something caught my eye. Standing back from the road, 'The Grand: showing today'. Were my eyes playing tricks? No, it was real! "A cinema and we live here! Dad, Dad, look at this can we go? Can we?" Of course we didn't. More rotten shopping! Just past the cinema there was another road. "Down there is your new school". It looked massive to us and nothing like our little village classroom, but at least I would be able to go past the cinema every day to get there.

So apart from finding a cinema and new school the only other memorable thing that day was going into the Co-op store. Nothing very special about that, in fact we went in under duress, but once inside I was suddenly aware of this strange overhead noise, then some strange object whizzing over my head. The shop had this amazing network of wires suspended from the ceiling and over each counter a canister like a tin can with a screw on lid and a large handle. It seemed that after gathering all your shopping and taking it to the counter, the assistant added it all up, took your money and put it in one of these tins which screwed onto the wire. He then pulled on the lever that was like a large trigger and the tin with your money in would go flying across the shop into the cashier's station. A few moments later the sound of a spring being released and the tin would come flying back to its starting position. Unscrew it and there would be your change. I had never seen anything like it before and could have watched it for hours, imagining Rob Roy escaping in one of these. The possibilities were endless, but nobody else seemed bothered so off we went home.

School day soon arrived and the entire household was a hive of activity. We had to walk to the top of the lane and catch a school bus that would take and bring us home from school each day. Everything was so strangely new to anything we had ever experienced before and to top it all the bus didn't go past the cinema to get there. It took a different route.

The school itself was to me large and foreboding and as soon as we got off the bus we were taken to meet the headmaster, a large man called

Mr Smith. After a pep talk of the school's function and expectations of us, most of which went straight over my head, I was separated from my elder brother whose lead I had been following. I was then handed over to a male teacher who took me through the front doors. Before me were rows of wooden slatted benches with coat pegs standing in rows looking like avenues of trees. We then went through a second set of doors with glass windows which led into a large hall with classrooms to the left and right. It was all a bit overwhelming after a small village classroom. We walked across the hall with heels clattering on the wooden floor. He stopped, turned the handle on a door and with a hand on my shoulder guided me in through neat rows of desks. All these eyes were looking at me and, oh how I wanted to run and fly off in my Biggles tree.

Over the days and weeks that followed it became apparent just how far behind I was in the learning process. Even at such an early age the differences from a village classroom to this were hard to grasp. My brother seemed to settle in more readily than me and I went into a rebellious stage. It was at the time the only way I could establish myself and be noticed by the others in the class, but of course you can't get away with that behaviour for long. My father was summoned to see the headmaster and I was ceremoniously marched in and given a lecture on learning and behaviour. If only old smithy could have read my thoughts Rob Roy was sorting him out for me.

Home-life had settled into a routine of school and playing in the surrounding fields and garden with our few newfound friends. We joined the Sunday school club and each Sunday afternoon would walk the two miles in whatever weather to get there. I even got a prize for attendance record, so how about that.

School life seemed to settle down as well although not my favourite pastime, so perhaps old Smithy's shock lecture in front of my father did have some effect.

We were told by our parents that on Saturday we would be going on a trip to Peterborough to visit Granny and grandad and oh how that week dragged on until Saturday finally came. Washed and dressed early, we all set out on this fine sunny morning and walked the three miles into town and waited for the bus. It was a red Double Decker. I had only seen them, but never been on one so blimey, another adventure. The bus duly arrived. The pushchair was stowed under the stairs and up we went to the front seat. It was one long bench seat and we all six fitted on with a clear view of what lied ahead. A strange conception. The view gave the impression that the bus was wider than the road and you could see so much it was just fascinating.

Winding along the country roads towards Peterborough and as we rounded the sharp junction at Ponders bridge we all thought we were going to fall in the river, but we didn't. As we neared the City the fields gave way to houses and shops and the road seemed to grow wider. As we stopped at a road junction with traffic lights, the first we had ever seen before Dad said, "Look over there. That's the football ground." (The Posh). The light changed to green and off we went again up and over the railway bridge. As we came over that an even larger bridge came into view. This one crossed a river. As the traffic in front slowed down we came to a stop in the middle of the bridge and had time to take it all in. To the left another bridge going across the river with a train going over it. Beyond that there were three large chimneys. "That's the power station where Granddad works," we were told. To the right of us was the Sea Scouts building and behind that an even larger building with the words Police Station over the door. Then I noticed it just by the river, The City Cinema.

Wow, just look at the size of that, but before I could say anything we were moving again and would you believe it, we turned away from the cinema, down by the river and into the bus station which was rows of lanes with numbers on posts. We drove round and stopped by one of these numbers, then I suddenly remembered this is where we stopped in the removal van some months ago.

We all got off, pushchair as well and walked into the city. The first thing you noticed was the noise and the traffic, but it was all part of the adventure and everything here seemed larger than life. The usual happened and we took it turns waiting outside while Mum or Dad went into shops, then at last it was on to another bus. Same routine again, upstairs to the front but this one was different. The gangway was down the middle with two seats either side and one of the front seats was full, but never mind, I still got the other one and the rest sat behind. Off we went again up the main street, eyes wide open, taking as much in as possible. The Town Hall with its large pillars and steps. The entrance to the Cathedral grounds. I could just see the market stalls on the other side, then round the corner and some more traffic lights. We stopped at the crossroad and ahead there was the sign 'The Broadway' another cinema, but this one looked even bigger than the one I had seen earlier. Whilst staring at this I suddenly spied right across the road 'The Embassy'.

This was getting too much for my imagination which, by now was running riot. Then with a jerk off we went again and as we drove past them I looked round at dad who must have known what I was going to say because before I had time to speak he just said, "Not today. Perhaps another time." Then, would you believe it, 'The Odeon' came into view and as we drew nearer the bus came to a stop right outside.

The entrance doors were set high from the pavement level about eight steps high and I could feel myself imagining what lay beyond those doors, but before I could conjure up an image, we were off again. We eventually arrived at our grandparents'. They lived in a pre-fab (that's a pre-fabricated constructed dwelling.) Many of these were erected just after the war as they made quick portable and affordable accommodation that was urgently needed for a short-term solution to the acute housing shortage that many cities faced. I remember my grandad saying on more than one occasion, "Freezing cold in the winter and boiling hot in the summer." Inside it was akin to a two bed-roomed bungalow. I liked it anyway. It was during one of these visits I met my uncle John. Although ten years my senior we just seemed to click, as you do with some people. As these Saturday excursions became more frequent I would look forward, days in advance to meeting him again, but as often as not he was never there. Never mind perhaps next time.

We had been in Ramsey just over a year now when, one day we were gathered together and told that there was going to be an addition to the family. After that, life seemed to settle into a drudge pattern. We hadn't been to Peterborough for a long time, mum was always poorly and dad spent most of his time at home. For us it was school then jobs when we got home. The only bit of light relief was going to the Sunday School Club I previously mentioned. It was a little chapel in the middle of nowhere. A two-mile walk, but we all enjoyed getting away every Sunday afternoon. Then suddenly and without warning our mother was taken away in an ambulance. Dad assured us all that everything would be alright and that the local post lady who we all knew well would be coming in to look after us so we all had to be very good and look after each other. As days went by and then weeks, Dad just coming and going and all the time, different people being in the house when we got home from school, it was a testing time. Then the day came when we were all sat down and told we had a baby sister and mum and the new baby would be coming home in a week's time. The event finally happened. An ambulance pulled up and out got mum carrying our new sister Janet. We all had a quick look, as you do, then off to our own pursuits.

Over the next few weeks we discovered that dad was no longer employed at the pig farm. It seemed he didn't get on with the pigs, so he was out of work and home every day. What we didn't realise was that the house we lived in was part of the work package, and we would soon have to move. After a few short months we were to have a Saturday trip to Peterborough again to show granny and grandad the latest addition to the family. I was so excited at the thought of seeing those cinemas again, but still hadn't been inside one for years and I was nearly ten now. It just wasn't fair.

It was during this visit that a turn of events took place that would have a major bearing on my life. I was asked if I thought I could find my way, on my own, from Ramsey to my grandparents in Peterborough. I of course cockily answered "Yes." It seemed that my granddad was a security guard at the power station and when he was on late shifts granny got very nervous and frightened of being on her own. They wanted me to spend some weekends there to keep her company.

Back home things had gone downhill, Dad was still out of work, arguments seemed more frequent. If it wasn't one it was another, in fact life was fraught and those immortal words came floating back, "When poverty comes in the door love goes out the window." What about these weekends at Granny's? No more had been said and I was getting really fed up with it all. I had rehearsed the route over and over again in my mind, and gone nowhere.

Then the day arrived, a Friday evening after school I was to catch the 4.30 p.m. bus that would take me to Peterborough bus station, then walk round the corner to the front of Woolworths and get on the number 29 that would take me to Gran's then do the exact opposite on Sunday evening, I know! I know!

So off I went on this big adventure keeping watch for all the landmarks I had mentally noted on our previous visits and in what seemed no time at all there I was. I had done it and was knocking on Granny's door; No 2 Shakespeare Avenue. What a weekend I had, spoilt rotten! No arguments, no looking after the little ones all trying to get some attention, everything here seemed so quiet and peaceful and the crowning glory was that I was sharing a bedroom with my uncle John. As I sat there well into the night enthralled by his stories of the current films that he was showing at the Princess Cinema and the work it entailed to project a film onto a screen I felt sure he knew just how much he interested me by the vast amount of questions I put to him. Just before sleep took over he said another weekend when you are here I will take you for a tour round the Princess. I drifted to sleep with the knowledge that I would be coming back.

The weekend was soon over and it was back to reality as I stepped off the bus back in Ramsey. My brother was there to meet me. On the long walk home I was eagerly telling him all about my weekend, but I don't think he was that interested. Mum and Dad listened to me relate the weekend's events between all the interruptions and shouting of the others, which seemed so much louder since I had been away, oh well, back to the routine and wait with eagerness for the next weekend away, I wonder when that will be, not too long I hope.

CHAPTER 4

Life at home settled down and was much the same. Dad was obviously out of work and any questions on that subject were met with, "He didn't get on with the pigs." The high spot during this time for me was a school challenge poetry reading of which I was to take part. The competition was being held at another school a short bus ride away on a Saturday morning, but as I didn't possess a school uniform one had to be borrowed for me. Off I went looking the part to read my poem in front of a panel of adjudicators – Walter De-La Mare's 'The Train' – I was a runner up, duty done, but I really wanted to be back in Peterborough.

Weekends came and went and not a mention, then it happened. "We are all going to Peterborough tomorrow. Would you like to stop over and come back Sunday?" I sure would!

Another weekend over and still no cinema visit. My uncle was away this weekend, so I had to satisfy myself with getting used to the local area. In Shakespeare Avenue there was a row of ten detached prefabs set back from the road with a pathway behind groups of small firs and bushes. Number 2 was the first one and at the bottom of a very long overgrown garden, a hole in the fence led directly into a children's play area, that was commonly referred to as 'the rec'! A slide, swings and a roundabout. One could have some fun in there. Halfway up the avenue it was houses then, as you turned the corner at the top there was a junior school and my aunt and uncle lived on the corner house. I would see lots of them in the near future.

The weekend was soon over and I was back home again. Nothing had changed. Kids loved to argue and make mayhem blaming each other for whatever, but only a week later I was on my way to Gran's again, happy as Larry! I could make the journey now without a second thought, well why not? I was ten! The weekend passed much the same as the others before. Friday evening listening to the Radio and 'Armchair Theatre', Saturday running errands and playing in the rec, but on this particular Saturday night, in came my uncle John. He had just finished work and would be here tonight. And as we shared the bedroom we sat up half the night whilst he told me all about the latest films until I could stay awake no longer. Sunday morning and quite out of the blue, he said "come on, get your coat on. You can come and see where I work.' Wow! I was ready in a flash and there we were, me on the crossbar of his bike, checking out the route for future use. If there was a Fish & Chip shop half-way down St Pauls road (I made a special note of that), then when we got to the end of the road the area seemed to open out. I noted and inwardly digested several shops, a pub called 'The Locomotive' this, I was told, was where we joined Lincoln Road. There did seem to be more traffic than I was used to which unnerved me a bit, but round the corner and onwards we went. The other side of the road I noticed a large play area then ahead of us a school 'Lincoln Road Secondary Modern Boys School' what a mouth full and it looked quite foreboding, but no matter, I wasn't going there! Just a little further on it came into view 'Princess Cinema' so this was it. As the cycle came to a stop I was off like a shot running around looking at the posters and the entrance doors, trying to peer in as my uncle John came forward with keys to the door.

In we went and once through the glass doors into the semi dark I could make out the sign Box Office and another saying Kiosk then lights around me started flickering on and all these shadowy images started to make sense. After a while of looking round the entrance area and taking in all the notices and displays, John said, "We are going up the projection room now. That is where I do all my work." Through this door at the side of the kiosk I followed him, up a flight of stairs into the Projection Room. With eyes wide open I just stood there trying to take it all in. All this black shiny equipment that stood twice my height rows of switches and the smell, one could get hooked on this. I later found out that it was the smell of celluloid and different types of film stock all mingled in the air. I was utterly fascinated with everything, "So this is what made the magic of film come alive," I said to myself. I knew more than ever that I wanted to be a part of it.

That first hands-on experience went by so quickly and I was soon back on the crossbar heading home to Gran's. As we peddled away from the Princess, John said, "You see that building over there, that's the New England Cinema. I'll take you over there one day to meet Len he's the projectionist there."

The rest of that day went by in a haze. My mind had been inflamed with all sorts of imagination from that experience and I kept taking out of my pocket the odd frames of film I had picked up off the re-wind bench, smelling it just to refresh the memory.

It seemed no time at all and I was back on the bus heading home to

Ramsey and mayhem, but this time I had something to tell them. The next few weeks slipped by in the normal routine, then one evening I was sat down in the room with just Mum and Dad.

What had I done? I didn't think I'd been any bother and I couldn't recall doing anything bad. It turned out that Granny had written to them asking if I could go and live there as Grandad had been put on a new shift system at the power station, where he worked as a security guard, and she was very frightened of being on her own. She would very much like my visits to become permanent. What did I think about the idea? It would mean a new school, but I had recently sat the eleven plus exam, and failed, which meant I would soon be going to a new school regardless, so I didn't see that as a problem. I was to think about if for a few days and they would talk to me again.

I thought of nothing else every time there was an argument, which was frequent in our house and something that never happened at Gran's. I could do my own thing, perhaps even go to the cinema on my own and watch a film, any film. The more I thought of it the more attractive it became so the date was set for two weeks' time. We would all go to Peterborough on the Saturday and I would stay behind.

The weekend did come round eventually and off we went, by the end of the day I felt many different emotions as I waved Mum, Dad, two brothers and two sisters goodbye. I suddenly felt alone and didn't really know why. I had spent many weekends here on my own before, but perhaps it was the realisation that I was splitting from our family group.

The feeling soon passed as I unpacked my belongings and settled down to wait for John to come home from work and tell me all about the latest films.

Monday morning soon came round and I had to go with my uncle John to enrol and start at this new school, Fulbridge Road Junior School. It was February 1958, a month before my eleventh birthday. My latter years of education were already mapped out for me by the failing of the eleven plus examination which I had sat at the school in Ramsey. My elder brother had previously passed and was eligible for a place at the Grammar School, but as things turned out he couldn't be admitted because my father was out of work at the time, so he had to be relegated to the local secondary modern school (snobbery or what?). After that there was never any pressure on me to excel in the examination, not that I would have done.

So back to Fulbridge Road and despite being only a month off eleven, the intake to a Secondary Modern School was from the ages of eleven to fifteen. The start month was September, so I had six months to pass the time away as the new boy at this Junior School (Oh what joy!)

My uncle John had by now left the Princess Cinema and moved to the Odeon in the city.

The next few weeks settled down into a regular routine of going to school which was only just up the road, running errands for Granny and getting to know my aunts and uncles as they nearly all lived in and around Peterborough. I did however manage a visit to the Princess one evening, but I can't for the life of me remember what the films were, but one of them was a western. I remember thinking to myself I would see it round to a certain scene then go home, only to have the queen suddenly come on., Oh dear I had sat through to the end of the day and had completely lost all sense of reality. A few words were had when I got home but nothing too harsh and it didn't stop me from a few more visits. Then came that fateful day when I ran all the way there with my 9d clutched firmly in my hand only to find a large sign across the front doors which said 'CLOSED'. In a daze and wondering what to do next I ventured over the road and down a side street to the New England Cinema. All was not lost, but on a reconnoitre of the frontage and a study of the programme displays I noticed the admission price was 11d. Despondently I walked back home re-living the memories of the few films I had seen at the Princess.

For what seemed an eternity throughout that summer of '58 when cinema visits were a non-entity, I spent my time getting streetwise to all the maze of back streets and the New England area, which included the railway sidings and parcel services. I spent many hours watching the steam trains shunting backwards and forwards and in the distance the main Northern Line where the express trains would go racing by. From the top of Spital Bridge I could get a good view and stand there wondering where they were going.

I got to know the New England area very well and would always make a habit to go past the old Princess, which was now being turned into Kennings Garage. A little way up was that Secondary Modern School I would be attending from September.

I made a few trips back home to Ramsey and the new found freedom I had meant that everyone was interested to hear of my away from home exploits, but I was always pleased to be heading back to Granny's and my new way of life.

My uncle John would keep me enthralled with a run down on the latest films he was showing at the Odeon and I would hang on his every word. Sunday nights was Top Twenty night on radio Luxemburg. We would usually congregate at my aunt Ivy's house just two minutes up the road because she got better reception, and religiously we would keep listings of any changes in the 'top twenty'. Dean Martin, Frank Sinatra, Perry Como, some of their songs would be in the number one position for weeks on end.

Life went on and September soon came. I started at Lincoln Road Secondary Modern School for Boys and soon got settled in. I made new friends, and learnt to know who to avoid and which teachers were more likable than others.

I spent Christmas at home in Ramsey and managed to get some time away and visit The Grand all on my own. No one else could see the attraction, but I had been starved of film for months and they made such an impact on me. I could relate events to a particular film title and this one was Danny Kaye in Knock On Wood so that was my Christmas made for me.

The year progressed and with March came my twelfth birthday. My uncle john, whom I did not see quite so often these days as he spent most weekdays away at his mates flat in the city, suddenly and out of the blue, one Sunday morning said, "I am going to visit Len at the New England Cinema would you like to come along with me," Silly question! Off we went.

The New England. I had often walked by it looking at the different posters each week but until now had never been inside. There was a double door entrance into a small lobby with a pay desk in the corner then up a flight of stairs into a foyer area with a single row of chairs around two side walls. The windows behind looked out across a playing field. To the left was the railway shunting yards and across the green you could see some of the shops in the New England Area. In the opposite corner was a pair of brown doors with a curtain across. That would be the entrance into the auditorium. In the opposite corner, another dark velvet curtain hung. We went through this and headed up a narrow staircase. A sharp turn then up again. It was getting darker by each step until eventually you had to feel your way along the small banister. At the top of this flight there was a door that led into a dark passage with an open door at the end. A chink of light shone thru as John strode off ahead. It was second nature to him, but I could only inch my way along following the sound of voices exchanging pleasantries. That smell of celluloid was steadily getting stronger.

Suddenly a light came on and flooded the passageway and there were voices of laughter "are you lost out there?" As I stepped up and into the projection room my eyes adjusted to the new level of light. There was just so much to take in at one glance, it was like gulping air with one's eyes! There were two large shiny black projectors which towered above me, rows of switches and levers. It was very much like I had seen at the old Princess. Then, as if suddenly to jolt me back to reality, John said, "This is Len who I have been telling you about." I turned round and stepped up into another narrow room which had a large crescent shaped window directly in front of a bench with winding handles and spools of film on. There stood Len. The smallness of the room made him look bigger than he really was and I looked up into this friendly smiling face, "Interested in all of this are you?" he asked. "Well go on and have a good look round." As he and John went on chatting about films, the Odeon and people I didn't know, I stepped back into the projector room and started to study all this wonderment, interrupting them with question after question. After a while they both joined me, as I was still taking in all this attraction. On the front wall, directly in front of each projector there were two windows, one higher than the other. "Portholes," I was quickly told in unison. "The lower one is where the film goes out to the screen 'the screening port' and the higher one is the 'viewing port'." The viewing port was way above my sightline even on tiptoe, then Len said these words that etched themselves into my brain, "Don't worry if you worked here you would have a box to stand on."

Len was perched on this high wooden stool and he sat there, filling his pipe and chatting away to both me (as if he had known me for years) and John, whom he had known for years.

I ventured back into this long narrow room with the window and gazed out at the view above the rooftops. You could see quite a way from here and I spied my school, a playing field, and Lincoln Road which was the main way out of Peterborough to the North. I could also pick out so many landmarks. I suddenly realised Len was standing behind me "Quite a view isn't it" he said as my mind came back inside and I turned over the winder handle. He obviously noticed me glancing everywhere with my eyes and sort of did a running commentary from wherever I looked, "This is the rewind room and is where all the real work is done." I didn't know the significance of those words at the time, but would learn what he meant much later. I pointed to this strange looking rack that went all the way across the end of the room. It had twelve narrow doors with numbers on. "Oh, that's where we keep all the reels of film," he said as he opened a door and drew out a reel of film, passing it to me. It was heavier than I expected and he started to explain that each film was made up of so many reels and that you had two projectors so you could change from one reel to another without any interruption to the picture.

I couldn't quite understand just what that entailed but got the general idea. At the other end of the room were piles of small boxes. "Those are the trailers of all the new films we have coming and these boxes are Day Titles." I was hoping I still look interested, but he had lost me a bit now.

Suddenly, out of the blue John called out, "Look at the time, we should be home for dinner now." So I picked up some film snippets off the rewind bench, said my farewells, with Len saying "you must come back up again sometime," and off we went down the stairs, which didn't seem so dark now, then into the top foyer. I took a quick glance at the Auditorium doors. "I never did get to look inside there, perhaps next time." I looked at all the posters of the forthcoming films as we went down the stairs to the front doors and I remember thinking "I wouldn't mind seeing all of those." Then it was onto the crossbar of John's bike and home for dinner. Wow! What a morning.

CHAPTER 5

As the weeks went by and no more Sunday morning outings I would ponder over the few film clippings I had brought home with me and recall in detail the events of that visit. Then the day came when I finally had 11d. The day passed so slowly with me just waiting for the first evening show at five o'clock. It was a double feature 'The Left Handed Gun' and 'Wind Across the Everglades'.

Paul Newman as
THE LEFT HANDED GUN

Plus

"A
WILD LAND
LIKE NO
OTHER...
AN ADVENTURE
LIKE NO
OTHER...

Burl Ives & Christopher Plummer

WIND ACROSS
THE
EVERGLADES

It takes 15 minutes to walk there and ten to run. I ran, through those familiar doors up to the box office window and handed over my 11d clutching my ticket it was up the stairs exactly as before but this time it would be through the double doors and into the auditorium. I kept looking around hoping to catch a glimpse of Len even if only to say 'I'm here' but it was not to be, so in I went and handed my ticket to a lady the other side of the doors. "Front four rows" she said upon inspecting my ticket, so I made my way down the aisle counting the rows until I reached the forth from the front. In the row I went, until I was centre of the screen. I had been told by John that this was always the best place to be. I tipped down the seat, a wooden one with no padding but that didn't matter. As I settled in and had a good look round, it wasn't as big as I was expecting but I had only seen the Princess and because that was huge I had thought that they all must be the same. This one was split in two halves. There were the front four wooden rows followed by a bank of approximately 100 seats, then the back half which went under a balcony set in three blocks with two aisles and a pillar at the front of each aisle. I estimated that there would be about 40 seats in each section, looking up to the balcony there didn't seem to be any seats, just complete darkness, except for the light shining through the four portholes. I sat there studying my surroundings when I suddenly caught a glimpse of Len peering out. I don't suppose he noticed me despite my giving a half-hearted wave. At this point the lights started to fade and on came the film. Paul Newman, the name didn't mean a great deal at the time but in later years I followed his films with affection as he was the first film star I saw at the New England Cinema. At the end of the second film it was time to go home, as promised, to my gran, as when Granddad was on night shift at the Peterborough power station I had to be in by eight o'clock. I didn't mind this as that was the reason I was here, living in Peterborough and I was really starting to enjoy it. I made it home in eight minutes, nice one.

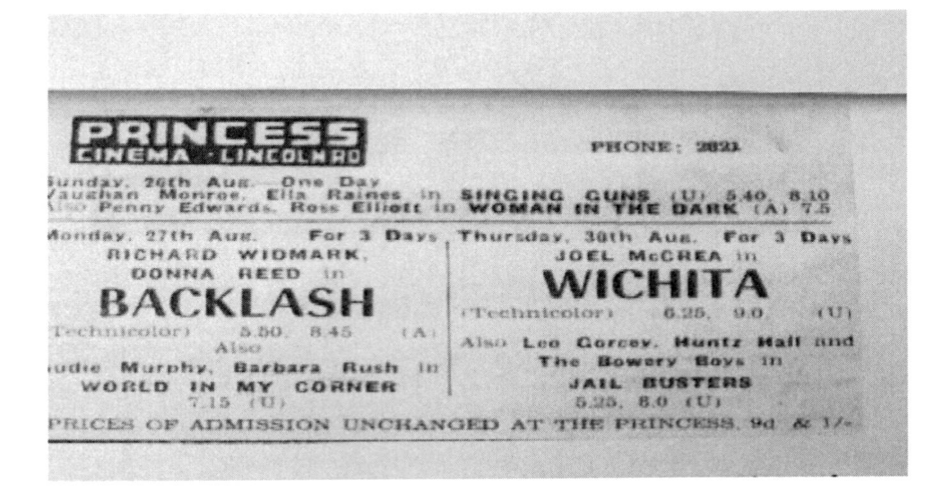

PRINCESS
CINEMA · LINCOLN RD

PHONE: 2821

Sunday, 26th Aug.—One Day
Vaughan Monroe, Ella Raines in **SINGING GUNS** (U) 5.40, 8.10
Also Penny Edwards, Ross Elliott in **WOMAN IN THE DARK** (A) 7.5

Monday, 27th Aug. For 3 Days
RICHARD WIDMARK,
DONNA REED in
BACKLASH
(Technicolor) 5.50, 8.45 (A)
Also
udie Murphy, Barbara Rush in
WORLD IN MY CORNER
7.15 (U)

Thursday, 30th Aug. For 3 Days
JOEL McCREA in
WICHITA
(Technicolor) 6.25, 9.0 (U)
Also Leo Gorcey, Huntz Hall and
The Bowery Boys in
JAIL BUSTERS
5.25, 8.0 (U)

PRICES OF ADMISSION UNCHANGED AT THE PRINCESS, 9d & 1/-

Osborne's Cinema / New England / Imperial.

NEW ENGLAND CINEMA

CINEMASCOPE

Sunday, Aug. 26th 4 Days
BETTE DAVIS,
RICHARD TODD,
JOAN COLLINS in
THE VIRGIN QUEEN
(Technicolor) 5.30, 8.45 (U)
Also Tyrone Power in
MACDONALD OF THE
CANADIAN MOUNTIES
(Technicolor) 7.10 (U)

Thursday, Aug. 30th 3 Days
KENNETH MORE,
VIVIEN LEIGH in
THE DEEP BLUE SEA
(Eastman Color) 5.25, 8.40 (A
Also Richard Widmark in
PICK UP ON SOUTH STREET
7.15 (A)
(Saturday at 4.40 and 7.35)

The very next time I saw John it was my turn to talk about a film he hadn't seen for a change. I also asked him if he would be visiting Len again soon and if so could I go too. He said, "Why not go on your own he won't mind and would be pleased to see you." I pondered on this for a few days then thought that as the cinema nearly always started at 5 o'clock I would get there a bit before and hang around for him to arrive.

The very next week I put my theory to the test. I arrived at the cinema about four thirty and peered in through the front doors. Complete darkness. Good I was there first. After a few minutes I looked around the corner of the building and there was this tall figure coming up the street. I knew instantly who it was and as he drew nearer, he noticed me and waved. I told him of my visit the other week and in return he gave me a run-down on the films he was going to show tonight. After unlocking the doors he beckoned me in and said, "Do you want to walk round with me whilst I get things ready?" So in I went watching his every move. We began in the box office where he started switching on some lights, then up those now familiar stairs and into the dark cinema. After switching on some more cleaning lights he said, "Now I have to light up all the secondary lighting. In case there is a power failure, these lights will stay on because they are gaslights." I watched as he went round to each light, turned on a gas tap, struck a match and lit the mantle. A bright beam of light was produced. After lighting five of these he said, "That's it, all done." In the quietness of the auditorium all you could hear was the sizzling of these gas mantles.

"Up to the box now," he said, "need to get that ready." So it was up that narrow staircase which still seemed as dark as ever. I just followed his footsteps until we arrived in daylight from the rewind room window. Once in the projection room he started putting on switches, pulling levers and then he started up both projectors. They seemed quite noisy as I tried to talk over them. It seemed that if anything went wrong it was usually when you first switched on after they had stood all day and they also needed a run to warm up all the moving parts or else the picture would flicker for the first few minutes and spoil the film.

Between the middle of the projectors were two large grey cabinets with lots of dials and switches on and a row of glowing valves. "That," he told me, "is the amplifier that turns the soundtrack on the film into sound waves and produces the different sounds."

After a while he stopped the projectors. Everything seemed so quiet again and then out of the film cabinet he produced a reel of film and took it over to the projector. I was totally fascinated just watching him twist this film effortlessly round a series of rollers and sprockets then onto an empty spool to re-fill as it ran through the projector. With this all done he put on a record and the sound of music filled the room. I managed a quick peep out of the lower porthole and could see rows of seats below and a few people settling down waiting for the film to start. Then Len said, "Better go and get your ticket it's going to start any minute." We said cheerio and he said, "Come and see me again." So off I went without mentioning that I had not got 11d for a ticket and was going home.

Over the next few weeks I kept this ritual up, there was odd occasions when I did get a ticket to see the show after our initial meetings. I got to light a gas mantle and put on a few switches in the projection room, all with Lens supervision. I even got a reel of film out of the cabinet and took it to him at the projector.

During these exciting times I had some weekends back at Ramsey and told anybody who would listen about my cinema experiences. Not a lot had changed at home. Dad was still out of work and I understood they would have to move shortly as the house was tied to a job he no longer had. My elder brother was joining the sea cadets and would have to come to Peterborough every Friday, so perhaps we would meet up sometimes. The only really memorable happening during the past months was when my dad came to Peterborough and I met him at the bus station. After dealing with the reasons he was there, we both went to the matinee performance at the Odeon. The film was 'The Key' starring William Holden. After the show had finished we both said goodbye and then went our own ways.

William Holden, Sophia Loren & Trevor Howard

THE KEY

It was now nearing my thirteenth birthday and I had become quite street-wise and knew my way around Peterborough and its suburbs without any worries. I was on one of my now regular visits with Len when he said to me, "How would you like to work here with me on two evenings a week?" If only he knew that I had been waiting to hear those words since that very first morning we met and he had mentioned standing on a box to see out of the porthole. So it was, "Yes please. When can I start?"

The usual running format for a second run suburban cinema was three programme changes per week. Sunday for one day, Monday for three and Thursday for three days, so he decided that I should work on a

Monday and Friday to start with that way it would be a new film each time. I could start next Monday. I ran home to tell Gran and Granddad, they didn't seem overly worried, only to point out that every third week Granddad would be on night duty and I would have to be in by eight o'clock, just make sure that happened and everything would be alright.

Monday couldn't come quick enough and there I was waiting outside when Len came round the corner and greeted me in the usual fatherly way. "I thought you would be waiting, well come on then." He unlocked the doors and into the darkness we went. Once we had crossed the small entrance foyer he reached out and switched on a row of switches and the staircase lit up. I was first up the stairs and waited in the top foyer for Len to catch up, then into the auditorium to light all those gas lights. There was just two I could reach without any help and he let me light them. Next up to the projection room which is where I craved to get to and I watched and studied his every move. Run the projectors to warm them up and get a record ready for the opening music. After a short time it was noticed that other people were in the building. That would be Mr Alderman the proprietor and the cashier.

At five o'clock Len started switching on more switches house lights, stage lights, and then the amplifier. That was when those large grey valves started glowing and there were those dials and meters that had been fascinating me. He reached over and started the record player, turned one of those dials and music burst forth from a speaker on the front wall. I could just see out of the lower porthole where the projection beam goes through and could see that the auditorium was lit up, and coloured lights splayed onto a blank screen. Some people were sitting in the seats. We were open and they were ready for us to do our bit to entertain them.

Both projectors now switched off the only sound was the music filtering through our speaker. "Time to lace up," Len said, "so go into the rewind room and get me Part 1." This I did instinctively, as I had been eyeing up the film cabinet which was all labelled parts 1 to 5. 'Never Steal Anything Small' and 1 – 6 'Whirlpool'.

James Cagney, Shirley Jones

In the musical comedy

NEVER STEAL

ANYTHING SMALL

Oh no, two part one's, which one would he want? I picked the nearest one and took it over to him, "Yes, that's the one," he said as I watched him thread the film around all those sprockets and rollers and onto an empty spool at the bottom. "Right" he said "now part 2 for the other one and we shall be ready to go," so we went through the process all over again.

At ten minutes past five he pointed out this large black knob which would slide up and down. "That is a resistor that fades the house lights up or down. We strike up the carbons by switching that large switch on the generator panel, turn that knob on the back of the lantern until the carbons touch then they arc together and produce a bright white light." As he did this there was a loud hissing sound as they touched then parted. "That's it," he said. "We are ready. Would you like to slowly lower the house lights?" I walked over and did just as he had described and watched the lights lower. As I was doing this he started up the projector and the film started to rattle through all those various rollers and sprockets. After a few seconds he pulled this lever that I hadn't noticed before and a beam of light went through the lower porthole and I could see on the screen the Censor Certificate which opened up every film. Whilst this was on there was a second sliding black knob which faded out the coloured screen lights. This done, I then noted him altering the dials on the front of the amplifier. "What are you doing?" I enquired "Oh yes. You turn this one down that fades out the record, switch over to film and turn it back up again." With this done he turned to me and said "That's it. We now have a picture on the screen."

I could hear the soundtrack, but couldn't see out of the viewing port. Len must have seen my frustration because he came in with an empty film case and placed it against the front wall. "Try that for size." I stepped up on to it. Oh yes, this was better. I could now see the picture, also anyone sitting in the front five rows. Up on the screen, there was James Cagney and I had helped put him up there.

In what seemed like no time at all Len tapped me on the shoulder and said, "I need to do a change over. Just stand over there and watch." A full reel of film ran for about 18 minutes and then you had to change over to the next reel without anyone noticing it. I watched and observed as this process unfolded before me. First the carbon arc was got ready then he did a last quick check over the film lacing. With an outstretched arm his fingers hovered over the on/off switch as he stared out of the porthole. After what seemed an eternity the fingers clicked down the switch the projector burst into life and then with a deft movement the light beam switched from one projector to the other as did the sound. With this done, the tail of part one was running through the projector as he just casually walked round and switched it off. Magic! Anyone downstairs watching this film would have no idea that this had happened, but how did he know just when to do it? A detailed explanation followed informing me that the end of every reel had printed within the frame a series of cue dots. The first was the projector start cue then, thirteen seconds later the next one was the cue to change onto the next reel. That was why each reel of film had a leader with all those numbers on it. We laced ours up with the number eight in the gate. By the time the projector had got up to speed the first frames of the new reel would arrive in the gate as the second set of cue dots appeared.

So now, whilst people were watching part 2, we had to get ready for part 3. "Firstly we need to rewind the reel back to the beginning that's your job, so get the full spool out of the bottom spool-box and take it into the rewind room." This I did with great relish and placed it on the re-winder. With Len standing over me I started to re-wind the film back onto an empty spool, letting the film glide through my finger and thumb so as to feel for any nicks or damage. This took some getting used to as it soon burns if you hold it too tightly, too loose and it falls out of your grasp, but with the amount of rewinding there was to do it didn't take long to master a technique of one's own. This job done, the reel had to be placed into the correct cabinet slot for its next run.

Part 3 was the next to lace up on the projector. Firstly, a clean down of the film path from any dirt deposits of the previous reel then lace up the new part making sure number eight was at the starting point. Next check the carbon lengths were enough to run the reel. I wasn't allowed to perform those tasks yet so had to be satisfied with watching his every move. This all done then you usually had about ten minutes left before repeating the process all over again.

Len with his Kalee 8

Open gears and chains.

The evening just flashed by and my head was so full of all the new things I had learnt and needed to remember for the next day, but I was soon brought back to reality as Len said, “Come on. It’s nine o’clock. Time you was on your way home.” I knew he was right and I would only be in trouble if I came home late, so reluctantly I put on my coat and said my farewells with the words “see you tomorrow” ringing in my ears.

Once home I would write everything down so as not to forget any of the thousand things spinning around my head.

The school hours of the next day dragged by slowly. The roundheads and the cavaliers held no interest to me and neither did algebra lessons. I sat there daydreaming the time away with yesterday’s memories still fresh in my mind.

At the end of the school day and what was to become the norm, I would rush home and do any little jobs my granny had waiting for me, then a quick bite to eat before running like the wind to the New England. I got it down to six minutes flat and usually just timed it as Len was walking up the street as regular as clockwork. He always left the house, where he lived with his sister and her husband, at four thirty, every afternoon. Together we would enter the cinema and the process would start all over again.

On only my second visit, Len let me light the secondary gas lighting. Armed with a box of Swan Vestas and steps to reach with, I went round lighting each in turn. As I was about to light the last one, I put the match too close to the mantle and it disintegrated before my eyes. Oh no! What had I done? My second day and the first job I'd been left to do on my own. I just stared in amazement as the gas light flickered and hissed back at me. I ran off in a panic to find Len and blurted out my dilemma, expecting a telling off. To my astonishment he just started laughing and led me back to the offending light explaining that a gas mantle, when getting old will often do this and mostly at the time the gas ignites within it which makes the white glow, but when the mantle breaks the air mixes in and makes it 'hiss' at you.

"Nothing to worry about," he assured me as he continued to teach me how to replace the offending object, still laughing at my panic-stricken reaction. "Come on," he said. "Let's go upstairs and get ready for the show." It was at that time I felt this bond between us and instantly knew I had found my niche in life.

CHAPTER 6

As the weeks flashed past, I now had money of my own albeit not a lot, but enough to allow a weekly trip into the city and watch a film, mostly on a Sunday as I was never required to work on that day.
On a Saturday, if I wasn't working and if Granddad was not on a night shift, I would catch the bus home and return Sunday evening. That way I could keep pace with all the home gossip and talk to Dad about my work and all the films I had seen. He was so interested in what I was doing and made me feel good about it that it was worth the trip home just for that.

It was during one of these trips that I was told my mother had now got a part-time job to supplement the household budget, but guess where? The Grand cinema as an Usherette. The Manager was a Mr Bill Hadden and the projection room was operated by his son Peter and during a conversation with my mother my name came into it as working in a cinema in Peterborough, he invited me to go and meet him on one of my weekend visits home.

I had just turned fourteen and despite the original plan to work two evenings a week, it never happened.

I was there every spare minute I had and the learning process was endless. I could now splice film together, lace up a projector and complete changeovers without any problem.

Proving my worth at the rewind bench.

Reminiscing over the past year, so much had happened. The family had moved away from the tied house into what could only be described as a camp enclosure with about six wood-constructed two bedroomed chalet-style dwellings, a left over from the war years and now owned by the council who used them as a staging post whilst waiting to re-house people. It was cramped and crowded to say the least, and I often found excuses not to go home for full weekends. My uncle John had left home and was about to get married. I would see him on my regular trips to the

Odeon as by this time he used to leave me complimentary tickets at the box office and believe me I took full advantage of his generosity.

You could often find me sitting at the rear of the circle. I chose this position because he would often come and take me into the projection room for a chat and a cuppa. I used to look forward to this and looking over some different equipment. It always seemed extra posh there as they all wore white coats and had the latest projectors. I was also getting to know other projectionists and was slowly becoming one of a group, but could sit and hold my own when telling stories of recent mishaps and new innovations.

I was, at that time, very interested in the three projector Cinerama process (more of this later). It was now 1961 and I had a full year working at the New England Cinema under my belt. I was totally hooked on films and when a normal programme would consist of a feature and a second feature film it was not unusual to see up to eight films a week. On a Sunday, when I wasn't needed anywhere else, I would be in the Embassy all afternoon, and then it was just a walk across the road into the Broadway for the evening, or the few hundred yards up the road to the Odeon, depending on who had the film I wanted to see.

I was still fitting in 'Granny sitting' and running her errands which seemed to fit in with my newly formed life style. School was not too bad. I got to know what lessons I could skip and the ones I couldn't, however I think I learned more from watching films than I ever did at school. I travelled the world on celluloid, and with only one more year of schooling left, that would do nicely. I never did really mix that much at school, though I had my favourite classmates and knew who to avoid, but as soon as I was out of those gates they didn't get a second thought from me.

The City cinema was situated near the river and was the very first cinema you saw when coming in from the west of the City. It always looked a massive building and yet I had never been in to see a film, probably because it only opened in the evenings and it was way out of my known route.

Unfortunately it was about to close and Len said he would take me to see 'Solomon & Sheba' as he would like to see a film there before its pending demise. On the Sunday of its final week we went and yes, it was just as massive on the inside with a wide sweeping staircase to the upper or lower circle. The downstairs was not in use anymore. We took our seats and looked around at all the neglect and decay that had been allowed to fester. No wonder it was about to close. It must have been close on 2500 seats in its heyday, but that was now a world away. The curtain raised, not opened. The only other cinema I had seen that happen in was the Broadway. The film itself was not that memorable, only the fact that I would never see another one in this cinema again.

One thing I do remember about the visit was nearing the end of the film when all these polished shields were turned into the sun and dazzled the opposing army into riding their chariots over a cliff edge. I turned to Len and said, “It’s like falling off Ponders Bridge,” (that is a bridge halfway between Ramsey and Peterborough and when you are on a double decker bus it gives the feeling you are going to drop over the bridge into the river). We laughed at the absurdity of it as we made our way home having said farewell to a passing cinema caught up in a dawning era that would affect us all in due course.

I now felt very confident in what I was doing and took on any new challenge with great enthusiasm. I travelled home for a weekend each month and became a regular visitor to the grand, either with my elder brother or on my own. It was on one of these visits that I was invited up to the projection room to meet Peter Hadden who had been asking after me via my mother. It was because she worked there that we got in for free, what a bonus, so after watching Tony Curtis in ‘Who Was That Lady’ I was shown up to meet Peter. After a formal introduction we just seemed to get on as if we had known each other a lifetime and of course I was interested in his projection equipment.

Projectors all have the same function, but no two projection rooms are the same, but the sound of film running through a projector never changes. Here he had a Kalee 12 set-up and the projectors stood on large concrete plinths that made them tower above me and I had to stand on the plinth to reach the top spool box. “How would you like to lace one up?” he said. The times I’d been asked to do this throughout my visits to different projection rooms. I passed that test with flying colours; little did he know I kept peering at the running projector to see where all the film loops should be. In no time at all the last reel had finished and it was time to go home, with a promise I would call in and see him next time I was home.

It was during this year that we were to all have a family holiday, something that had never been done before. A week in Great Yarmouth and I was included. For the weeks ahead this became the main topic of conversation on my regular visits home and soon the time arrived. That Saturday morning was like a scene straight out of a Carry On film. A family friend (‘Cuffy’ was the only name I ever knew him by) had this reliant three-wheeled van and we all piled in. Three adults and five kids plus luggage. For the life of me I can't now visualise how we did it, but we did and we made the journey to the North Deans caravan site.

The excitement between us all was unbelievable, a great big adventure was about to be had.

All piled into this three wheeled Reliant van

Pete and me at Yarmouth

Family holiday, everyone happy.

The family

Dad with his Youngest daughter Janet.

Our one and only FULL family holiday, what fun we had!

After the usual unpacking, Pete and I went off to explore the site. Communal shower blocks and toilets, the shop and the clubhouse and the route down to the sea front. Being the eldest of the brood we were allowed to go our own way and stay out later and my we had some fun. In fact everyone did in their own way. I managed to see Robert Mitchum in 'Home from the Hill'.

Robert Mitchum & Eleanor Parker in

HOME FROM THE HILL

I also saw a variety show with Arthur Haines, because that's what Pete fancied, but it wasn't as good as my film.

It was my last year at school, which had just become an intrusion to my watching films and working at the New England. Every event in my life was marked with a film title.

My uncle John, who was now married to Betty, coerced me into taking her younger sister Margaret out on a date. Bloody hell! I had only seen that sort of thing in films, but here goes. It was off to the Embassy with a box of Milk tray and Margaret to see Tom Courtney's debut film 'The Loneliness of the Long Distant Runner'.

Tom Courtney *-in-*

THE LONELINESS OF THE LONG DISTANCE RUNNER

Just like the title, it was a long old night and after I had taken her back home I had to kiss her goodnight on the doorstep. Then I ran like hell all the way home and I have never seen her since, although I did ask after her at a family funeral meeting last year.

Back at the New England I was in my element learning how to mend seats and do numerous maintenance jobs around the cinema which also included pasting up posters each week on a billboard up Lincoln Road. Some light relief came in a missive from the local fire authorities that any cinema with Nitrate film in stock should have it disposed of by the fire department as it was now deemed to be a dangerous substance. Len had often told me stories of this type of film stock and how highly flammable it was. I had also seen pictures in the trade magazines of film catching fire should the projector suddenly stop or the film break in the picture gate. The concentration of heat from the light source would instantly ignite the film and the flame would travel up the film path into the top spool box which in turn could actually explode despite all the fire prevention traps installed on the projectors. These only delayed the inevitable, this type of film stock was phased out from the early 1950s onwards, and I had never worked a Nitrate copy, but the time had come to completely outlaw the commercial use of this dangerous film stock and to comply Len and I were searching through some metal cases in a store room looking for any of this old film. We found about a thousand foot in total (that's approximately 10 minutes of film). Len decided it wasn't worth bothering the Fire Department with such a small amount and we should take it out the back of the cinema and burn it ourselves, so this we did. He split it into three smaller rolls and out we went and unrolled some of it so we had a long trail then the roll. It looked just like those films I had seen where they lay a trail of gunpowder. With a match, he lit the end of the film and off it went, this bright orange flame streaking along the ground and the acrid smell given off which according to Len was more dangerous than the actual fire. As the flame reached the roll of film it just seemed to burst into life and shot this orange flame up into the air. "That's what I was telling you about," said Len. "That's Nitrate and goodbye and good riddance to it."

Now, unbeknown to Len, I had got just one frame of this which I put in my pocket and later that day I was to play a prank on him. He smoked a pipe and I slipped this frame of film under the newly laid tobacco completely unknown to him and waited for him to light up. Eventually the inevitable happened as he placed a lighted match onto the tobacco the frame of film ignited and shot the tobacco out like a miniature explosion. I thought he was going to have a fit he went white then red but thank goodness suddenly saw the funny side of it. That was his very last brush with Nitrate film.

The stage end of the New England was a magical place of an era gone by. A small orchestra pit was set into the stage. Where the piano was sited during the silent film era, it was now full of seat spares, then behind the screen in the dusty dark corners old pieces of antiquated equipment were stored I used to take a torch and spend many an hour looking these over and having a play with the sound effect pieces. The Thunder Sheet, which was a large sheet of metal hanging from a rafter and depending how fast or violent you shook the rope it would simulate rolling thunder quite realistically.

A big old church bell that sat on the floor and boy did that echo around. Another strange piece was this large black unit that was 'sound on disc' it still had a disc on it which said, 'The Indian Squaw Reel Six'. It seemed this was the forerunner of film soundtracks and the disc played from the centre outwards and if any frames within the reel became damaged they had to replace the exact number with blank film to stop the sound going out of sync, but nobody complained as your favourite film stars were actually talking to you.

The crème de la crème was the Powers No5 projector complete with turning handle and front flicker blade shutter. I used to take an old trailer length film roll back stage and wind it through with a torch, projecting a picture onto the back wall, just to practice getting a constant speed. It meant nothing to anyone else but me. I felt like H G Wells's Time Machine going back in time.

Weekend back at home and the Grand this time. It was Cary Grant in 'Operation Petticoat'. I must say things at home seemed to have improved greatly. Mother was still working at the Grand thank goodness as it kept my film intake up. Dad had finally got some work with the local council as a street cleaner. There seemed to be a lot less tension now. My brother Peter was in his last term at school and had got himself a Saturday job at the local baker's shop. He was also committed to the sea cadets and had applied to join up at sixteen. As for me, I was still wrapped up in my own little film world, averaging out at around thirty films a month and was becoming a common face at the three city cinemas, often getting in on a 'freebie' as I now knew most of the projectionists. Gerald, who worked at the Embassy and would often call round to visit with Len, would often leave me a ticket at their box office. He even took me for a tour of their projection room. That was an experience.

The Embassy had by far the largest auditorium of over 2000 seats and a full stage which was turned over to Christmas Pantomimes and some variety shows throughout the year. The rear circle was very steep and seemed to go up and up to meet this row of portholes which were almost ceiling level.

Once I entered the projection room it was noticeable the angle or rake of the projectors, Phillips FP7's with water-cooled gates and magnetic stereo sound was the first vision I had of this overpowering equipment, the room itself seemed to go forever with a row of spotlights they used for stage work and all those portholes situated about waist high one just looked straight down at the screen, it gave one an unrealistic sense of proportion. It was certainly an eye opener for someone from a second run suburban cinema, but on hearing stories of all their problems with this fine looking equipment it didn't seem quite so overpowering.

The screen was some 300 feet away so the light source had to be sufficient to reach the distance, but the heat generated by these carbon-lit arc lamps meant the film path had to be kept cool by running water through plastic pipe-work along the film path. The problem came when several of the rear circle toilets were flushed at the same time, and this often happened. The water pressure would drop and the projectors would heat up very quickly. The film would start to buckle and then lose its focus. As for the magnetic sound system, it was explained as a nightmare. The soundtracks, left and right, were printed along the film edge. A brown magnetic strip, very similar to a reel to reel tape recorder. The problem was that it was very easy to de-magnetise the sound track, hence your film would be playing along nicely, all the sound effects enhancing the patrons' enjoyment of a good film, until suddenly crackles and bangs would come out of the surround speakers instead of proper sounds because the track had been wiped. It was, of course, these early experimental systems that have given us the advancement into digital sound of today, but right then and there I was pleased to let the Embassy have the headaches over the latest technology.

Some of the films I did see there were impressive with their superior sound system. 'Journey to the Centre of the Earth', 'GiGi', 'Mutiny on the Bounty' (the sound broke down the night I went to see that), 'Summer Holiday', etc.

Across the road at The Broadway a complete change, but fortunately the Chief Projectionist there was 'Wilf'. Would you believe that he was Len's brother? It seemed strange that Len had hardly ever mentioned him, so I did not press the matter, but having made myself known, I was invited into the projection room. Another eye opening experience. The Broadway box office/kiosk was open to the pavement and passing public, with double entrance doors either side. At the rear of the kiosk, at ceiling height there were two small windows and now and again you could see someone walk by, but just their legs. This vision had fascinated me on my previous visits. During my 'invited' tour, it turned out that the projection room was situated directly behind the kiosk and the first thing to take my notice was that the projectors were pointing upwards, the first I had ever seen at this angle. Wilf must have noticed the expression on my face and explained that the projectors were situated under the circle and shot upwards to the screen. This reminded me of the Sunday night I had been in the circle watching a film only the week before with Trevor Howard in 'The Clouded Yellow'. It was quite a smoky atmosphere and I couldn't work out why I was looking through the light beam instead of having it over me, but now, I knew.

The projectors were the latest Kalee 21s, the streamlined version that I spent ages looking over in the trade books.

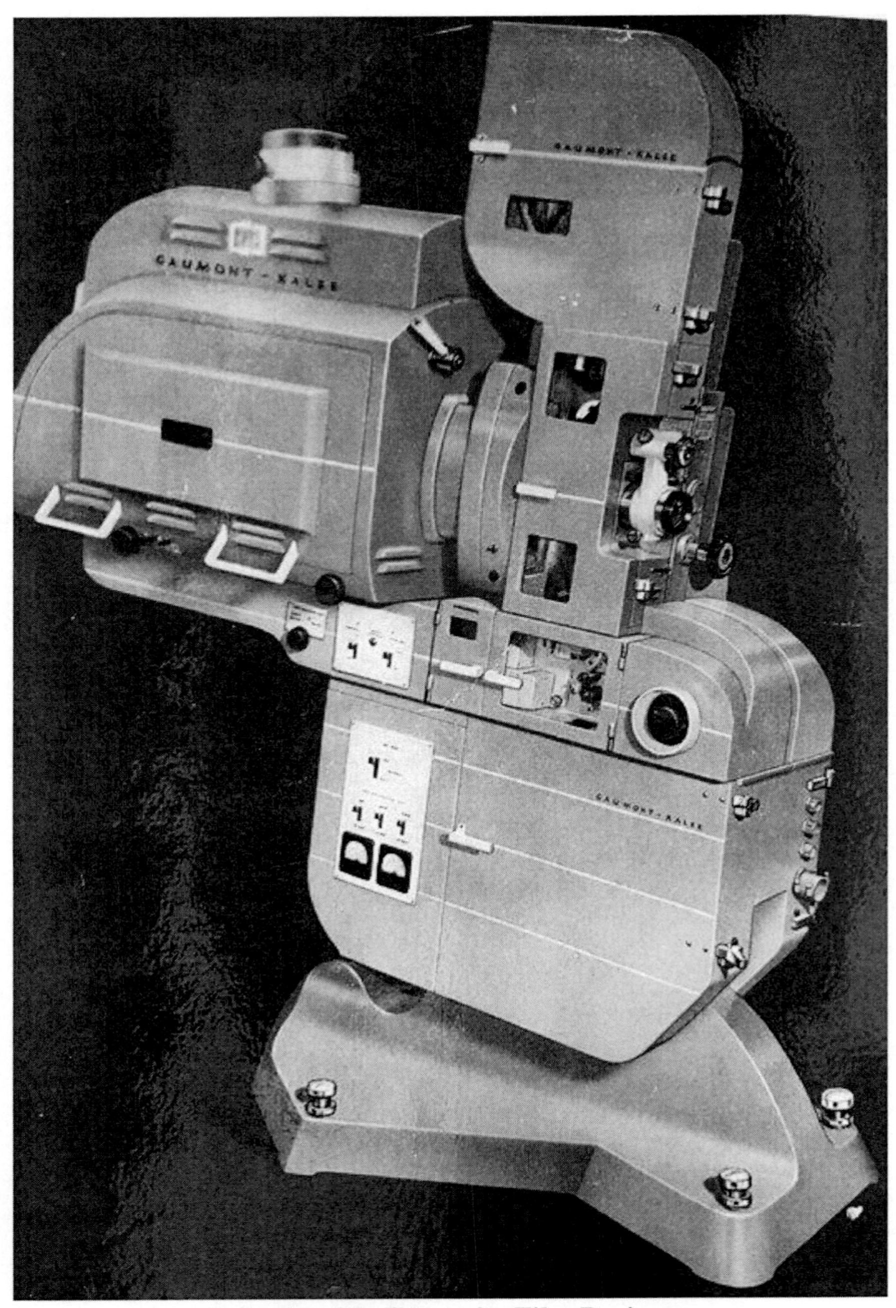

Kalee 21 - My Favourite Film Projector

The projection room was very small compared with the Embassy and Odeon. In fact the top spool-box almost touched the ceiling. I was told it got very hot during the summer, but they could open those windows. “It must have been your legs I had seen whilst getting my ticket,” I said to him. He didn’t seem amused, but explained that with the windows opened you could look down and talk to the cashier and kiosk girls, although you had to be kneeling on the floor to do it.

Back at the New England, I was telling Len all about my visit. Although, as I have said, he had mentioned his brother in earlier conversations he did not seem as impressed as I was and I got the distinct feeling that they didn’t converse very often. I thought it best to drop the subject.

CHAPTER 7

Another weekend at home and another visit to the Grand, this time with my brother Peter to see John Wayne in 'The Horse Soldiers'. Afterwards a visit to the projection room, exchange some trade gossip and then escort our mother home after the show.

The year flashed by at record-breaking speed. I could now run a show from open to close unaided and I really felt part of a team. Checking through my year journal I had seen 346 films during 1961, some of them several times over. I was competent at doing small DIY jobs around the cinema. The only blot on my landscape as 1962 got underway, was the fact that I would be leaving school at Easter on my fifteenth birthday and the schools careers officer was busy getting work placements set up for all those undecided, at either Baker Perkins or Peter Brotherhoods, the two main industrial factories of Peterborough. I had made it clear that I was only interested in working in cinemas but as there were no vacancies at that time and I could not leave school without a job to go to, it was a stark choice. Either accept an apprentice job with one of those or stay on at school until September. Both options filled me with dread and I poured my heart out to Len, who cheered me up by saying, "Let me see what we can do." That statement certainly made 'The Devil at Four O'clock' and Frank Sinatra more entertaining than films had been of late.

As the deadline drew nearer and I was still none the wiser as to my direction, Len and Mr Alderman called me into the rewind room, away from the noise of the projectors and proposed a plan of action as best it could be. For two pounds ten shillings a week I could have a job there. They would give me a letter to this effect for my careers officer. However, I had to talk it over with my granddad. 'Right, leave it to me.' It was just the news I had been waiting for.

This promissory letter was my proudest possession, until I showed it to my granddad who instantly hit the roof. He ranted on about Perkins, the need to be an apprentice in such a modern factory, the future being in diesel engines and of course that they would pay six pounds a week. If I didn't fancy that then I could go to Brotherhood's, another large engineering firm. He just couldn't understand that this was not for me and stormed off out to the pub, leaving me quite bewildered and wondering if John, his youngest, had had to suffer the same rant. Granny, good old meek and mild Granny, who could see how upset I was, just quietly said he'll be alright when he comes back home, and he was. After about ten pints, he had decided that my future was up to me. That was Granddad. My fifteenth birthday was soon upon me and to celebrate it, leaving school and starting work full time, Len brought in a birthday cake and some drink, which went down really well along with Cantinflas as "Pepe" running in the background. I really felt that I had made the right decision. I even had this photo taken on that day.

Cantinflas -as-

My fifteenth birthday, and a new white coat like the Odeon projectionists had.

My first ambition, once working full time, was to get a bicycle. Len said he would buy it for me then I could pay him back at five shillings per week, so the deal was done and off we went to a bicycle shop on Lincoln Road. I chose a Raleigh three speed chain enclosed model, with front hub dynamo for the lights. It was the first time I had owned anything brand new and I was chuffed to bits. I could now get around independently.

A work rota was made up for me to follow. This was something else new to me and as the cinema only opened from five o'clock it seemed strange to have a shift in the morning, break for the afternoon, then be back for the evening.

Len, a confirmed bachelor lived with his elder sister and brother in-law, and I spent many afternoons with them doing odd jobs and running errands. It soon became a second home.

At weekends, when I was not needed I would get on my trusty cycle and pedal off the fourteen miles to Ramsey. No one ever said, "You can't do it," or, "You are too young," it just seemed the natural thing to do. I would set back on a Monday morning and be back at work by ten o'clock, come rain or shine.

The morning shifts taught me a whole new insight as this was the time when the cinema was all still and quiet and there was time to do all the regular maintenance jobs. Stripping off rollers and sprockets, checking for wear and giving them a good clean. I learnt the internal workings of a projector and what a 'Maltese cross' was. It had been explained to me but I never until now grasped the importance. Len had previously explained that all you actually saw was a series of still pictures, but how could that be? I had witnessed horses and motors chasing across the screen. They were not still pictures in any imagination, but on stripping down the internal workings of the intermittent movement there was a special gear shaped like a 'Maltese cross' hence its name. On one of its four points there was a striker pin that attached itself to a shaft that had a sprocket on the working side of the projector. He demonstrated to me how all the other sprockets drove the film through the projection path in one continuous movement. This sprocket, 'the intermittent' only turned one quarter of a revolution as the striker pin came into contact with the sprocket drive shaft. This sprocket would always be found at the base of the projector gate. The gate was aptly named as it opened just the same with two runners either side for the film to glide through and an aperture for the light beam to project a film frame situated between the lamp housing. There would be a shutter blade that was synchronised to the intermittent movement and as the striker pin moved down one frame of film to cover the aperture the blade of the shutter would cut off the light source then as the film became stable the second movement of the shutter would let the light through until the striker pin's next movement. All this being done at the rate of twenty-four frames every second and the film loops top and bottom of the picture gate would stabilise the erratic movement and keep the film free flowing. It was this amazing succession of still frames projected at speed that gave the illusion of movement. See what I mean? You learn a little something every day and I was perfecting my part in this illusion.

In March 1963 my parents moved house and at last had the chance to settle in a large four bedroomed family council house in the heart of Ramsey. As my elder brother Pete was now at HMS Ganges a naval training base, I arranged some mid-week time off to help with the move. I spent Monday evening showing Stephen Boyd as 'The Detective' then cycled home as promised. The next day it poured and poured and it was four o'clock before we managed to start the move, this time in an open-backed lorry from a friend of a friend. Know what I mean? We all mucked in and got the job done and it was pleasing to see them all settled in to their new abode and I had mixed feelings when it became time to peddle back to Peterborough.

The year settled down into a routine that suited me just fine, Granddad had now retired so I didn't have the pressure of being in at certain times and became my own person. It seemed that if I wasn't busy showing films I was in some other cinema watching them and that was just fine by me. This idyllic life went along merrily for about eighteen months when suddenly Granny was taken poorly and then into Hospital and life moved into another phase. Granddad spent more time than ever in his local pub 'The Locomotive' and I would often pop in there to see him and, despite being under age, have a pint with him and get the latest update on Granny's illness which turned out to be worse than I had at first realised. I remember getting very upset at being told her illness was terminal and she was going to spend some time with John and Betty when released from hospital. This duly happened and I now found myself completely alone away from work.

Granddad seemed to have taken refuge in his local and on the occasions I did meet up with him he was either well and truly sozzled, or very mournful.

I had now been working full time for eighteen months and could run the show single-handed and would often do that whilst Len had a well-earned evening off. I completely immersed myself in the celluloid world I had become so familiar with. It was during this time that the proprietor, Mr Alderman, decided that we would no longer open on a Sunday as it had become a weekly battle with the local bovver boys that only saw cinemas as a playground to wreak as much damage and havoc in as they could get away with. This was something that was going on in all size of towns and cities during the early '60s and he had seen enough of his cinema being vandalised in this way. Again the old saying of "when one door closes another one opens" comes to mind as he was approached by a Mr Singh a local 'Indian' businessman who wanted to hire us on a Sunday to show Indian language films for his countrymen, so our Sundays took on a whole new role.

From the projectionist angle it turned out to be a nightmare. We had never experienced this type of film before. To give you some idea, in those very early days Cities that had Indian and Pakistan communities would obtain copies of films direct from their own countries and move them around from venue to venue, mostly in the boot of a car. These films were normally two and half to three hours long (approx. Ten reels) and the general condition was often horrendous after being mauled over by anyone that could find a venue and someone to show them. The film would usually turn up late Sunday morning for a two o'clock showing. Len and I would haul it all up to the projection room praying for a good clean copy, but alas it was nearly always an unmitigated disaster area. There would be all these cans of film with no English markings on, no leaders or tails, we just knew the first reel and the last. Some reels would be in shreds where the last show had broken down with it so many times and then just wrapped it around the reel and taken it on to the next poor unsuspecting sucker. Poor old Len would be pulling his hair out, what was left of it, throwing tins all over the place. I remember this Mr Singh coming into the projection room during one of these tumultuous moments, all turban and beard with a big grin and in broken English telling us not to worry. As long as it was a picture that could talk and sing to them everybody would be happy and off he went not knowing or wanting to know what a problem this had become to us.

Len wasn't in the habit of having our film breakdown umpteen times during a show and he wasn't going to start now, but who was he kidding?

After a couple of hours of splicing broken film and trying to trace the continuous sequence of frames from one reel to the next, we would have some kind of resemblance of a made up film ready to show. At two o'clock the cinema would start to fill up with an assortment of folk all speaking in foreign languages of different dialects Sikhs, Hindus, Pakistanis. To us it was just a wall of noise all this excited chatter, it must've been the focal meeting point. Then it would be time to start the show. Most of this film stock was extra thick and would rattle through the projector with the many joins clattering through and the dialogue jumping about. There was no way of telling how many frames were missing from each join. These films didn't have any subtitles so we never knew what was going on and had no way of following any type of story content. Just when you thought you were getting somewhere it would break into song for about five minutes and you would be back to square one. Towards the end of each reel the cue dots of all shapes and sizes would start to appear we would just take a guess start up the projector and change over reels between words. Each time we did a change over, Len would say "How was that? Did it look like a follow on?" To be honest, I couldn't tell, but the audience were still all watching it, quite content so it must've been OK. Then – bang – a join would break on going through the projector and film would come spewing out onto the floor. If the break was at the bottom of the projector it was sometimes possible to get it back on the spool without stopping, but this didn't happen very often. It was usually below the film gate where the most pressure was. In a situation like this, the film breaks and the intermittent sprocket can't feed any film through the picture gate and the frame just freezes. Seconds later all you see on screen is the picture bubble up in the intense heat of the carbon arc light. There is no choice but to stop the projector, re-lace the film and have a restart.

On these occasions all we could hear was the hullaballoo from downstairs. "More haste, less speed," Len would say. More often than not, when a film breaks it's usually for a reason. This film stock had become brittle due to age and constant use, so once laced back onto the projector the restart would cause it to break again sometimes this would go on for several attempts until you could get to a stronger portion of film. The more noise that seeped up from downstairs the worse you seemed to perform. Mr Singh would come running in most excitable, "What is the matter? What is the matter?" as Len would be frantically tearing off lengths of brittle film and throwing it across the room. Mr Singh would then make a sharp exit muttering something we couldn't understand. Once up and running again, we would wait anxiously for the next breakdown. Len would sink onto his stool and have a pipe of swan, and this is how our Sundays seemed to be for a while.

Then this one time an excited Mr Singh came in special to tell us he had acquired this brand new Indian film which would show next week and it was in colour and starred the latest Indian hero. The film was 'Hercules' or at least the Indian equivalent. The next Sunday soon came, and the film, against all our doubts turned up on cue. Fifteen reels, all in colour and in good condition. We just couldn't believe our luck. At the usual two o'clock the place was heaving, standing room only. Len was even polishing the portholes and lenses ready for the off. Once given the go-ahead we shot the first reel. It looked really good on screen arrows flying everywhere and plenty of singing which always seemed to go down well. However, half way through reel three everything ground to a halt and all the lights went out. Len looked across to me and said the immortal words "I don't believe it! It's a power cut."

After just a few minutes the increase in noise from downstairs came flooding up. Pandemonium was the best description one could give and we kept well out of the way. Poor old Mr Singh, he had to give everyone their money back, but he would bounce back, and he did.

Granny never did come back home and I would call in to see her at John and Betty's. She had a room of her own on the ground floor and was always in bed. It didn't take a lot of working out that her hourglass was running out and very soon the news was broken that she had passed away peacefully in her sleep.

A few weeks after the funeral it became obvious that we could not go on living in this way grandad was drinking heavy and we would just pass by on occasions. Then came the day that my parents made a visit, and to cut a long story short it was decided that my grandad would be moving in with them. Therefore I would have to move back home as well. There was no other choice. I couldn't commute to and fro and my earnings were nowhere near enough to make me self-sufficient. A date was set and it seemed that my world had come to an abrupt end. What was I going to do? Len, didn't want to see me go, but could offer no alternatives and we would talk for hours about what I would do with myself once I had left his care. Then suddenly, out of the blue and without warning a letter arrived from a Mr Hadden at the Grand Cinema Ramsey. A projectionist's position had become available and if I was interested would I call in and see him on my next visit home. See what I mean about doors opening and closing?

It transpired that my mother, who no longer worked as an usherette at the Grand had often spoke of me when chatting to Bill Hadden or his son Peter who was now running their sister cinema in Huntingdon. She had told them I was coming home to live, so an interview was set which really was just a formality. They needed a projectionist just as much as I needed the job and a start date was set. It wasn't going to be so bad after all. Len sent me off with his blessings and his usual words of wisdom and I had to promise to visit him whenever possible, and so the next chapter of my life started to unfold.

1964. Our Pre-fab home was being run down and I was moving back home straight away as the starting date for my new job was imminent. Granddad was to follow on in a few weeks' time as he too was moving into the spare bedroom with Mum and Dad. Dad, being the eldest, thought it his duty to take care of Granddad in his hour of need.

The end of the week soon came and I was paid my last wage from the New England along with a little bonus and a thank you note, that was nice. I didn't really want to go, but knew I had to. With a few bits and pieces that I would immediately want, I pedalled off into the sunset, so to speak.

CHAPTER 8

Sunday 8th April 1964 at the appointed time of four o'clock I met Mr Bill Haddon at the doors of the Grand cinema Ramsey.

Grand projection room

Grand auditorium

Although I had been there on many occasions as a customer and as a visitor into the projection room, I could not help but feel very apprehensive as I followed Bill up the stairs to his office to collect my very own keys to the building and instructions about the evening's show. From then on I was on my own, as I unlocked the projection room door and walked in.

The first thing I found was a welcome note from Peter and a guide to where all the switches and controls I would need could be found. I suddenly felt at ease and although on my several earlier visits to this area I had taken stock of the equipment layout, it was now just a matter of familiarising myself with enough to start the show. The projectors were Kalee 12's with Gaumont arc lamps. Luckily I had, during my previous visits, laced film onto these and taken a change over, so I felt quite relaxed as I walked around switching different pieces of equipment on. The doors were due to open at five o'clock so that was my deadline to be ready. By that time I had houselights and coloured footlights all on, background music playing and reel one laced up and ready to go. The next ten minutes seemed like an eternity and if I checked everything once I did it umpteen times, then as if by an automatic reaction at ten past five I fired up the arc lamp by touching the positive and negative carbons together. With a crackle and hiss the bright flame given off was adjusted to a one-inch gap for maximum illumination. Then it was time to fade the houselights down and the curtain footlights halfway and whilst these were fading, start up the projector and let the numbered leader run through. The film certificate followed this and as it went through the projector I opened the dowser across the light beam and let the light onto the picture gate and, if all had gone to plan, the certificate would be showing on the curtains. Open the curtains and fade off the coloured lighting. This done it was now time for the sound. Fade out the background music, switch over to the film sound track and fade back up for the opening film company trademark. All done. A sigh of relief and the show was underway. Another check round to make sure everything was running smoothly and then I had about sixteen minutes before changing over to reel two. That was my first night at the Grand and the film? Oh yes it was Audie Murphy in 'To Hell and Back'.

THE EXCITING TRUE LIFE STORY oF AMERICA'S MOST DECORATED HERO

AUDIE MURPHY

TO HELL AND BACK

The Grand, being a rural independent cinema had to trade in films well after the city centre release dates. That wasn't so much of a problem in the early sixties as feature films were not shown on television as a regular feature, and there were no Video or DVD outlets, so the time delay from its initial release to being shown in the smaller cinemas was not too critical. I did soon become aware that the Grand was even further behind than the New England and when looking down the list of forthcoming film titles I noticed that quite a few titles I had already shown at the New England, 'Zulu' being one of them, another of my favourites, so I could look forward to that, then 'Mutiny on the Bounty', another epic with Marlon Brando and Trevor Howard.

This was one of the first films I saw at the Embassy in Peterborough in stereophonic sound, but it broke down half way through, and I did feel sorry for them as several members of the audience were cat-calling and making wise cracks. I felt like shouting, "Shut up, they are doing their best!" Another film I heard in this format was 'The Sundowners' and that was fine. See what I mean about every film making a mark on one's life.

Living back at home, settled down into a routine over the next few weeks, Granddad moved into the spare bedroom and seemed to be quite content with his new surroundings. I even managed to talk him into coming to the pictures to see 'Mutiny on the Bounty' with Mum and Dad; that was a first. I don't think even he could remember the last time he watched a film.

The year was passing by at a pace and the Grand was to put on wrestling once a month to combat the dwindling audiences. My part in this operation was to install the overhead portable lighting, so whilst the ring was being erected, I would be above the ceiling lowering cables to haul up this large lighting contraption that would illuminate the ring.

Bingo evenings would be my night off, thank goodness, and I would often pop over to Peterborough and pay Len a visit. I did notice that he was not looking his old self just lately but he assured me he was OK.

Having been at Ramsey now for a full year I was becoming increasingly bored with the routine of the job and apart for the few incidents to liven it up, such as lacing up the wrong reel six so when it became time to change over from reels five to six poor old Sean Connery in 'Woman of Straw' became a black and white 'B' movie, until it was rectified. If a projectionist makes a mistake however minor, it is noticed straight away, and I have made my share during the years.

February 1965 I received a message from Mr Alderman the proprietor of The New England saying that Len had been taken ill and he would like to see me and put forward a proposition, so on my next day off I went to see both him and Len. It transpired that they would like me to go back to the New England and run the projection room and, with Len's behind the scenes guidance, book the films until such time as Len would be well enough to return.

I had very mixed feelings about returning. Was it a backward step after being away and proving myself elsewhere? However, they did a good job in selling the idea to me saying that I was the only one who could save the day, etc., etc., and as a further incentive Mr Alderman would put down the deposit on a new motorbike for me to travel on. How could I refuse that?

A start date was set and I returned to the Grand and tried to explain that I would be leaving at the end of the week and returning to Peterborough. They were not best pleased with me to say the least and both Mr Haddon and his son Peter tried everything to make me change my mind, but it wasn't to be and for the last couple of days they all just stonewalled me and I was made to feel uncomfortable.

It was those parting days that made me leave without any regrets. I couldn't get away quickly enough.

On the Monday morning I bussed into Peterborough and met with Mr Alderman at a pre-arranged destination and we drove to Colin Hinkins Motorcycles where it was decided the best machine for a new rider would be one of these Honda 50 motor bikes. They were new on the market and had built in leg guards and they would throw in a Perspex windshield.

I had some practice rides on a plot of waste ground at the rear of the shop, all went well and the deal was done and I cautiously made my way to restart at the New England Cinema.

I very soon settled in and it seemed that I had never been away. The days flashed by so quickly as I had much more to do. We changed films twice a week. We would run Monday for three days then Thursday for three days. That format never varied and of course the Indian shows on Sundays. There was always film handling work to be done, along with film booking, publicity ordering and displaying in and off site.

In the 1960s we had the dreaded 'British Quota' book to keep a check on. It had been decreed by the government that to support the British Film Industry all cinemas would have to show a yearly quota of 'British' product, but the problem was there just weren't enough British productions to sustain the quota, so we would log anything that had a BR/E registration number. If you didn't keep check on this you would end up during November / December showing mostly British 'B' movies before the yearly returns were sent off.

God bless the Mining Review, if anyone can remember those. They were a twelve-minute documentary film produced by the coal board for showing in the mining areas and working men's clubs and unless you had an avid interest in coal mining activities most were a twelve-minute bore.

They were a monthly issue and 'British Quota' as was 'The Edgar Wallace Mysteries' or 'Edgar Lustgarten from the Annuls of Scotland Yard', so with all that and film timings and press adverts to draft and send off each week, the days were fulfilling to say the least, and one had a sense of achievement.

I used to see Len several times a week and could tell he was not getting better, in fact just the opposite, although he still had an interest in what was going on at the cinema, and was always ready with some advice on the complexity of film booking.

Suddenly one realises that six months has just flashed past. I was more or less just Bed & Breakfast at home. Six months and I hadn't had a day off yet then, out of the blue, I was told that Granddad was going to move back to Peterborough. He was not settled in Ramsey and missed all his local haunts. I think this was the first time he had ever been out of the City so it was understandable and he had the offer to move in with another of his sons. Thinking back now that was the last time I ever saw him.

CHAPTER 9

Half a year passed and I suddenly felt in a rut. It was obvious Len wasn't ever going to get better. The cancer was taking its toll and despite his enthusiasm I suddenly felt trapped. It was also now becoming a realisation that any kind of modernisation to the old cinema was just a pipedream and probably a ruse to get me back. My poor old Honda 50 was just not up to the job of a thirty mile round trip every day and would often cough and splutter especially when it had a head wind, then wham! One fateful Sunday evening heading home, at the city centre crossroad I misjudged an oncoming car and he hit me broadside on. As I lay in this shop doorway waiting for an ambulance I suddenly felt so alone and despite being battered and bruised, I started to ask myself what the hell was I doing? Working all the days, come what may. I had no mates or buddies; in fact I was a real loner. That is what the job had turned me into, a film junkie! It had become my staple diet and at eighteen I had come to this crossroads in my life, in more ways than one.

It took me a week to get over the accident but now my next dilemma. No transport. My poor old Honda had been taken back to the motorcycle shop and my next job was to bus over and find what repairs were needed. There it was, lying in a twisted heap having just been written off by the insurance man, so it wasn't going to work out too bad after all. It meant I wouldn't have to wait for repairs and could get fixed up with a new machine straight away. I chose a Honda '90' this time, the next step up and the only one I could afford the repayments on. A phone call and Mr Alderman stood guarantor for me once again and was pleased to do so, as it meant I would return to work pronto, and relieve him of doing the projection room. I also had a faring fitted for extra weather protection, and it all looked very sleek as I rode off, back to the routine.

My first port of call was to see Len who by this time was confined to bed and looked a pitiful sight. As I sat holding his hand I could suddenly see myself in years to come. Len had dedicated his life to being shut away in a projection room year after year and I had been groomed to do the same. Time to go and get the show ready. I left with the promise of returning very soon, and of course being careful.

It took me two days to get my projection room back into order, as is often the case when someone else stands in for you, now doesn't that sound sad and the talk of a loner? The good thing to come out of the accident, well two good things really, I was to get every Tuesday as a day off as it was decided that fatigue was the main culprit of the accident, and I had this new and better machine which would zip along nicely. All I needed to do now was to take a driving test and get rid of these 'L' plates.

Tuesdays came and went and I seemed like a fish out of water. My brothers and sisters had grown up without me noticing them, and had their own friends. Probably, because I lived away during their younger years, we slightly lost the daily touch.

Dad now worked in the Officers' Mess Kitchens at the nearby RAF Upwood and seemed very happy with his lot. Mum was doing several Part-time jobs around town until an opportunity arose to also work in the Kitchens, so all was well and happy at home, and oh yes, guess what? They both now had Honda '50' motorbikes.

It was on one of these off days that I went to see Cecil Hart. He ran a small independent cinema in Whittlesey. I had got to know him through his visits to Len a year or two earlier and had always promised to go see him but never had. Then, out of the blue he rang and asked me to go for a chat and a look over the place, so there I was standing outside the small town cinema showing Frank Sinatra in 'None but the Brave'.

Frank Sinatra in

NONE BUT THE BRAVE

Cecil spotted me and came bursting out as if I was his long lost son. After the cordial chat and tour of the projection room it transpired he wanted me to go work for him. Thanks, but no thanks. This was no different than what I was already doing and even I had come to realise that the days of these small independent cinemas were numbered. They were closing all over the country, even alongside some of the larger ones. We parted company with the usual pleasantries, and I never did see him or the long gone cinema again.

November 1965 I duly took my riding test, and failed. I now had to wait six months for another one.

As the year was drawing to a close my every thought was what to do with myself. It was obvious the old New England was hanging on by a thread, as was Len. To Mr Alderman it had all just become a hobby, and I suddenly felt trapped by it all. If it hadn't been for the feeling of loyalty, some days I could have jumped on my machine and rode off into the sunset, that John Wayne influence again.

I spent weeks scouring over the situations vacant columns in the trade magazine 'Kine Weekly'. I did really fancy this new form of technology that was all the rage in the mid '60s – Cinerama.

Fascinated with this new technology

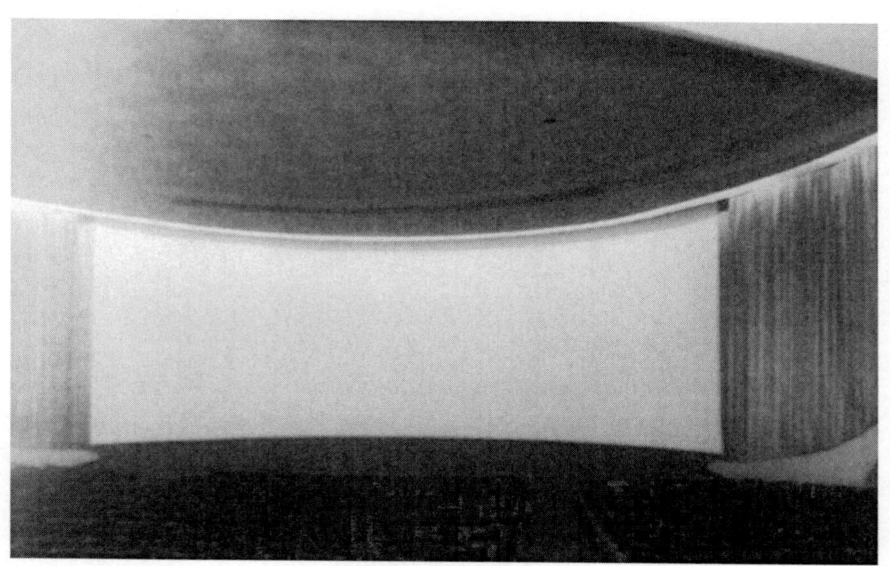

What a screen

It was a three projector system where you projected onto a massive curved screen. Each projector covered a third of the screen area. The big film of the time was 'How The West Was Won' and as there were very few venues with the capability of screening such films they would run for months at a time.

I found a job vacancy for a co-chief projectionist in Bristol, so why not? You couldn't get much different than that! Without further ado I wrote

off after the position, a couple of weeks went by then this rather splendid envelope turned up with the Cinerama trade mark emblazoned on it, thanking me for my interest but the position had been filled. I'm not really sure whether I was disappointed or relieved, the thought of Bristol was another world away, so back to the drawing board.

Christmas came and went, then I caught this advert for a second projectionist at the Abbeygate Contemporary Cinema Bury St Edmunds. Where? Out with the map and it looked promising, not too far away. I put pen to paper once more, again within the week I was told the job had been taken, but thank you for your interest we would keep you on file. A couple of weeks went past. It was a Sunday morning. I was working in the projection room spooling on Sean Connery in 'The Hill

SEAN CONNERY

They went up like men!
They came down like animals!

THE HILL

when the front door bell (which rang in the projection room) burst into life and made me jump out of my skin. As I made my way down from the top of the building, cursing the disturbance, a complete stranger stood at the door and introduced himself as Doug Kenton the Chief Projectionist from the Abbeygate Bury St Edmunds. It transpired that the person they took on for the vacancy backed out at the last minute, and as my letter was most favourable would I still be interested? After the usual guided tour of the projection room (a recognised procedure between visiting projectionists) I got to like the freshness of this person and agreed to visit him at the Abbeygate on my next day off, at the arranged time of 2 o'clock.

The following two days dragged by and every spare moment I had was taken up studying a road map. At twelve o'clock on the appointed day the adventure began I was on my way and as the miles went by the landscape started to change from the flat fenland to the leafy trees and rolling countryside. I was soon in Newmarket and following the signs for Bury St Edmunds along the A45 which seemed never ending. I kept memorising the different landmarks for the journey back home, then as I came over the brow of a hill, there in front of me was Bury St Edmunds. As I followed the only road into the town centre I decided to ask for directions. I did this several times before finding my way to Hatter Street and the Abbeygate Cinema. It was, as previously described to me, a large residential looking building halfway down a side street off the main thoroughfare with a larger than life sign that you couldn't miss when you turned the corner.

"ABBEYGATE". To the left of the entrance there was a large green door that led into a lobby which was for the residents of the several flats that were also part of the building called 'York House'. I could put my motorbike in the lobby whilst I had my interview. This all done and now thawed out from the journey, I proceeded back out into the street to have a good look around. Six entrance doors flanked with the current programme details. Bette Davis in 'The Nanny' and the next presentation starting Sunday would be George Peppard in 'Operation Crossbow.'

A NEW HIGH ADVENTURE
Sophia Loren, George Peppard

OPERATION CROSSBOW

Inside, the foyer was neat and tidy with two-tone grey tiled flooring. To the left were the box office and kiosk and directly ahead, four marble steps led up to a highly polished area with entrance doors each side. There was a poster frame in the middle with a flower arrangement below. To the right there were a set of double doors with the words Cloakroom on. After taking all this in I proceeded to the box office where the cashier, a small grey haired lady had been eyeing me up. I had noticed this since entering but not until now had made eye contact with her.

I introduced myself by asking for a Mr Kenton and was completely taken aback when she said "You must be Pat. I was told to expect you. I will let Douggie know you are here." I suddenly felt so at ease and all the apprehension just faded away.

By the time those cloakroom doors opened and Douggie came through, I was raring to go. After the usual pleasantries he said "Let's go upstairs and have a cuppa." Nothing could have been more welcoming and homely, so I followed him through those doors into a lobby with several rows of coat pegs. A door ahead was marked Office and another one was marked Staff Room. A third door, in the corner which we went through led into a small kitchen area then out into the open yard. We proceeded up a stone stairway to the next level. Upon entering I heard that familiar sound of a purring projector. It's a distinct sound that film loops make and no matter what make of projector that sound is music to the ears of any projectionist and without looking you always know your film is running true to form.

As I followed him through a door to my right he said, "You can put your coat in here." At a first glance it was quite a compact area with a workbench, a vice and several bits of repair work waiting for attention. Next to that was a large black object humming away to itself. That was the rectifier that turned the power supply from AC to DC current that was needed to run the powerful arc lights. Down one end were two chairs, a cupboard and table, the brewing up area as it was known. As we stood in there chatting whilst the kettle was being put on I really needed to see into the next room. When at last we did move off, due to a reel change being needed, I again followed through the next door and into this long narrow room. The projectors were situated first. That would be about the centre of the auditorium, the best place to project a picture from so as to get a good square image on the screen. Next to them, a smaller piece of equipment that looked quite alien to me. It was a slide lantern which was used for putting messages up on the screen and could be projected on top of the film in cases of emergencies. Beyond this was a larger observation porthole with a polished wooden box fixed below. Lift the lid and there was the record player that was used for all the incidental music. Next to this was a high stool, of course that would be the most comfortable position to view the film as it was lower and bigger than the projector port holes and you could lean on the box work. Over the years I would watch many films through here, but today my very first vision was of Bette Davis giving her most sinister look as 'The Nanny'. The rest of the area was taken up with an L-shaped rewind bench, two rewinders and film racks underneath. Another doorway led off in the far corner. It all looked very functional. Whilst I had been taking all this in Douggie had done a routine change-over of reels and came walking up to the rewinder with the used reel under his arm. He handed it to me and said, "You wanna rewind it?"

"Sure, no problem!" So away I went my first test I think. You see, there is a knack to rewinding film and letting it glide through your fingers, so as to feel for any split perforations that require attention. Miss these and your film would eventually break whilst running through the projector. Also you needed to keep the edge of film even so as not to have any proud layers that could get bent over whilst transporting to the projector. This was another cause for film breakdowns. On average you could easily rewind about thirty reels of film during a working day so you soon found your own way of doing this. Each reel would take about three minutes to rewind, then with the end tucked in, it would be placed in the correct numbered compartment and await its next showing. The now empty spool would be placed on the rewind part of the rewinder and be ready for the next one. With that done the now familiar voice said, "Would you like to lace up?" so taking the next full reel out of the cabinet I walked over to the empty projector and had a good look at it. A Kalee 12.

I was familiar with these from the Old Grand at Ramsey, but as I threaded the film through the various traps and rollers down to the soundhead I realised I hadn't seen one of these types before. British Acoustic, several rollers and film clamps. 'Which way?' I thought to myself. Douggie was up the rewind area so didn't see my initial panic, and then Len's advice came back to me. "If you get stuck, walk round and look at the other one." Of course, easy! I completed the task, wound the film onto the bottom spool and inched down to number eight in the film gate, just the carbons to check now. Peerless Arcs. I had never worked on these before, but I had seen them at the Embassy in Peterborough. I opened the door and checked there was enough carbon, both negative and positive to run another reel. I had noticed a chart on the back wall where you could measure the length and it would convert it into film minutes burning time, but just a quick glance told me there was plenty for the next reel so mission accomplished.

Douggie came over and did a quick once over, adjusted the size of a film loop, no importance, just for the sake of doing something I reckon, and we now had about twelve minutes to go before the next reel change, so into the rest room for that cuppa then back to the tests. This time a changeover - that's when one reel finishes and the next one starts, something I'd done a thousand times before, but it's always a bit daunting for the first time on different projectors, especially when your every move is being watched. The changeover went without a hitch. Mission accomplished. Good old Bette Davis didn't know the difference. That's how the rest of the afternoon progressed.

I was to meet the Manager, Mr Berry, at five o'clock. It was his day off, but as he lived in a flat adjoining the cinema he would see me then.

Well before the allotted time I already knew that I could settle very happily here and make my mark. After being shown to the residential area via those York House doors, up a flight of wooden stairs onto an upper landing, Doug pointed to a door and said, "That's where I live at the moment. Mr Berry lives down the end of the corridor on the right and that other door goes to a flat up above." What a maze of a place. A ring on the doorbell and it opens almost immediately by this very friendly looking person who almost appeared to be waiting for that ring and was ready to pounce. With the initial introductions over Doug made his way back and I was invited in to the living quarters of the cinema manager. After yet more tea and a getting to know you style of chat it was down to business. If I decided to take the appointment there was a member of staff who took in lodgers and had a vacancy until I got settled. It certainly seemed that all had been prepared in advance and I was expected to take up the offer.

Also, with the eleven pounds ten shillings per week, how could I refuse? At the New England I was getting six pounds a week so this seemed like a king's ransom and all too good to be true.

The date was set for a week on Sunday, 16th February 1966. It was now six thirty and how time had just flown by. I bid farewell and made my way to give the news to Douggie, who genuinely seemed as excited as I at the prospect. Another cup of tea before I made my way home. I Watched the trailer reel. Next week's presentation was 'Operation Crossbow' and I wouldn't be here for that but the week after was 'Sands of The Kalahari', so that would be my starting point.

THE STRANGEST ADVENTURE THE EYES OF MAN HAVE EVER SEEN!

SANDS OF THE KALAHARI

The journey back home on this clear frosty night soon passed as I had a million things spinning around in my head. My worst problem was going to be telling Len I would be leaving and moving away. I hadn't even told him of my interview as he was now quite poorly, and would never recover from his illness. Arriving home Mum and Dad were anxiously waiting to hear my news and I went through the day's events as meticulously as I could remember them. They were genuinely pleased for me and assured me that I had made a good choice and wouldn't be that far from home.

Back at the New England things didn't go down quite as well when I explained to Mr Alderman my decision to leave. I tried to explain my reasons for doing so, but he would not hear of it. He claimed I was ungrateful and that I had let him down at a time when he needed me most, but I had made my decision and so I just wrote a letter stating the facts and I would finish on Saturday the 15th February. Nothing more was said on the subject, in fact very few words were ever spoken between us again. He would send up the cashier, Mrs Debeau to try and talk me into changing my mind. As if?

Len was a different kettle of fish the one person I had been dreading to tell and as I sat at his bedside he just said, "I knew something was up and I am not surprised." He asked so many questions about my interview, the cinema and projection equipment. I think he would have come too, had he been well enough.

I left him with the promise of seeing him again before I departed, of course I would, and I did, the following Saturday. With a tear in his eyes he said goodbye and squeezed a five pound note into my hand as a parting gift. that was the last time I saw Len, my mentor. He passed away two months later.

CHAPTER 10

Sunday 16th February 1966 was a bright, dry and sunny day for mid-February and I was up at the crack of dawn. I just couldn't lay in bed any longer. I washed and polished my motorbike, went and filled up with petrol and it was still only ten o'clock. My worldly belongings were packed into a suitcase and strapped onto the carrier of the bike. I had planned a one o'clock set off time which should get me to Bury about two thirty. I would meet Douggie at his flat and get directions to my new digs, then be at the cinema by the five o'clock Sunday opening time.

By twelve I was saying my goodbyes and on my way. I couldn't wait any longer. As the different styles of countryside passed me by, I could remember certain landmarks of my previous journey only two weeks ago and on that final stretch, that long straight rollercoaster road between Newmarket and Bury St Edmunds I really let my bike go on the downhill straights. Then, without warning, BANG! I lost all power and slowed to a standstill. "Oh bugger, I didn't bargain for that." 'More haste less speed' came to mind. I had often been told that by Len. After an engine cooling off period I limped the rest of the way on half power. I was later to find out the exhaust valve had blown. But here I was at 1.30 p.m., standing outside the Abbeygate.

My new workplace

The Abbeygate interior

Feeling quite pleased with myself as I parked the bike and made my way up to Doug's flat. A ring of the bell and the look of surprise on his face as he opened the door. "You're in good time," were his opening words. "Come on in and meet the rest of the family." Marie with that fascinating Suffolk accent that was new to my ears and David, his six-year-old son. They all made me feel so welcome. The next hour flashed by then Doug said, "I will take you to your digs now. I'll bring the car round and you can follow me. That will be better than giving you directions. It's 28 Derwent Road up on one of the estates. Margaret Warren and her husband, Bill. A nice couple. See what you think. At least it will get you settled in."

Off we went and as I followed his Ford Thames car down all these narrow back streets I thought to myself 'I shall have to find my way back later.' We went across town, under the railway bridge and down this tree lined road, into an estate. Still keeping note of the turnings and landmarks, after a few more twists and turns we pulled up outside a row of houses. 28 Derwent Road. This was it. They must have been waiting as the front door opened before I was off my bike and this motherly looking lady came out to greet us. In the doorway stood Bill. I had to look twice as he was a spitting image of William Bendix, a character actor who was in many films of that decade. After the introductions Doug left us to it by saying don't rush back, just ease yourself into it. With my suitcase off the bike, I followed them into their house, a maisonette. I was soon made clear of that as I was shown around. I would have the back room as mine and share the rest of the rooms with them. I could park my bike under my window round the back. It all seemed very nice and inviting, in fact who could have wanted for more?

After tea and cake it was time to find my way back to the cinema. I had been given the back door key in case they had retired by the time I got home as Bill had to be up at six o'clock, he worked on the American Air Base at Mildenhall. They both wished me a good evening at the cinema and off I went.

The evening just flashed by, I didn't even have time to watch Stanley Baker come to grips with Stuart Whitman in 'The Sand of the Kalahari', but I learnt so much about the cinema and its workings that evening. The one duty I wasn't prepared for was that it was the projectionist's job to maintain the heating within the cinema and during the mid-evening interval I was shown round to the back of the building and led through a door which went directly down a concrete staircase. This was the boiler house. As I reached the bottom of the steps the heat met me and directly ahead was this monstrous looking object with doors, pipe-work and temperature gauges all staring at me. "Grab that shovel" Doug said "and use it to knock open the fire door." This I did and for as far back as I could see into this cavity were red hot embers. "Put half a dozen shovel fulls of coke on it," came the instruction. I looked around behind me and there was this pile of coke. "It's not too bad at the moment" he said. "When we start getting low it's a lot further to walk with it." I dug the shovel into the pile and started back to the boiler. "Try and get it to the back" I was told. A good swing and shoot it off the shovel. BANG! The corner of the shovel caught the door opening and the coke shot everywhere. Doug just burst out laughing. "You'll soon get the hang of it." I just stood there staring at my empty shovel, the sweat trickling down my face. "Half fill it, shut the door then make your way back," Doug said. "I'll go and start the show." He chuckled as he made his way back up the steps. After a while I completed the task and made my way back to the projection room where it was explained that the very first job in the mornings was to de-clinker the boiler and set it going for the day. I was really looking forward to that in the morning.

Douggie at the Abbeygate projector

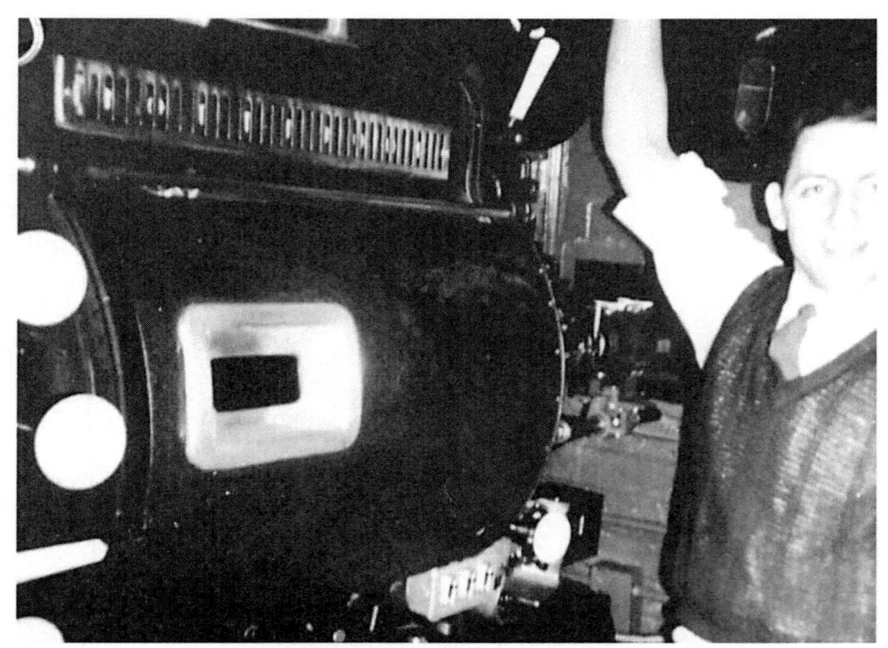

My very first day and all was well with me.

My very first evening came to an end much sooner than I had wanted it to, but we started switching all the different systems off and made our way down to the foyer area which was now in semi darkness and minus any customers. Mr Berry was making his usual final checks before exiting the building, but tonight no one seemed in a hurry to leave. We just stood around chatting about ourselves in turn, when suddenly it was noticed that it was past eleven o'clock, so a hasty goodnight was made all round and I was making my way to my lodgings.

I turned off the engine well before arriving and quietly pushed it round the back and gingerly let myself in the back door. There was a cup and sandwich with a note telling me to make a drink and feel at home. What a lovely thought I was thinking to myself, when the door opened and in came Mrs Warren (Margaret) from then on. I was trying to apologise if I had woken her, but it turned out she was lying awake listening for me to make sure I had got back alright.

Margaret could talk for England and this seemed like it was going to be a long session. I was right, it was. I finally fell into bed at 1.30 a.m. and thought over the day's events and what a day it had been. It was about then I knew that coming to Bury St Edmunds had been the right thing to do.

Back to the cinema at ten o'clock, just let myself into the projection room with my new set of keys and then get busy cleaning down the projectors. It's amazing just how much dirt and dust particles come off a reel of film and if it's not cleaned down on a daily basis this is when you start scratching the picture area. These particles build up, get warm then turn very hard. As I was doing this job in came Doug rubbing his hands together. It was one of those bright frosty mornings. "Let's go and sort this boiler out and get some warmth into these radiators. Leave that job till later. Oh, by the way we have a row of seats that were ripped out of the floor by the yobs last night. We'll need to fix them before we open."

Again, we went down to the boiler house. After opening the fire doors it was plain to see that there wasn't a lot of life in it. I was shown how to handle this eight foot long poker that was used to break up the clinker that had formed overnight, then with this other instrument, which can only be described as a giant pair of tweezers, you drew out a piece of clinker and placed it into a metal dustbin. After doing this several times and trying not to breath in the dusty fumes given off from these glowing hot pieces, you were left with a shallow dull lifeless firebase. "That's the worst bit done," I was told. "Now you need to switch the blower on that pumps air under the embers and sparks them back into life." As if by magic, small flames came flickering through those embers. "Right, just put a couple of shovels full on then we can leave it for half hour, then we'll come back and bank it up."

With that done, it was good to get up, out of that dusty old room and into some fresh air again. This was going to be a morning ritual throughout the winter months.

Before I knew about it a week had just flown by. I had managed to send a postcard home letting everyone know that all was well. I had managed to find a motorcycle repair garage to get my bike repaired. It would be nice to go on full power again.

The lodgings turned out to be very homely and I felt a part of the family, having been out for a drink with Bill and Margaret and in return, I did a couple of maintenance jobs around the house for them.

The programming at the Abbeygate was of the standard format. Sunday One day. These were usually a double bill programme of some old re-issue films, mostly clapped out and in dreadful condition. It was no wonder the Sunday night yobs took to wrecking half the seats. It must have been out of shear frustration. It sure as hell frustrated us in repairing them every Monday and we always noticed that if we showed anything of interest, our seats didn't suffer.

Monday for three days. These were usually films of a lesser calibre. In the 1960s and early '70s Motion Pictures had no other outlet but cinema, so every film distributor played hard bargaining to get their film stock on screen, no matter what the content. It would often be the case that to be able to show the 'good' one you would have to take several of their second rate ones as part of the deal. These films would get used up there whilst the better quality ones would be saved for Thursday, Friday and Saturday. The Pathé Newsreel would be changed twice weekly Monday and Thursday.

Should a BIG film come out, it would run for the six or even seven days, but very rarely any longer as it would always be brought back at a later date then re-issued the following year. After that, it would most likely appear as a double feature programme. It was nothing unusual to start the last performance at around six thirty and run till ten thirty. That was the normal programming for cinemas across the country during this period. The one exception to this was Easter 1966. 'My Fair Lady' we were to run this for two weeks (with the exception of Sunday's). It was going to be our first real biggy of the year and we wanted to make it special. Our manager, Mr Berry was an organ enthusiast and it was suggested that during the intermission he could play his Hammond organ for the fifteen-minute duration each show. He jumped at the chance to perform to a captive audience, so we set to and built him a platform made from wooden beer crates and plywood covering in front of the screen, then proceeded to heave down his organ from the flat above. Job accomplished, we fashioned a spotlight out of the old slide projector and we were ready for the big event. I must say it went down very well, made the local press and became a talking point about how it made the evening's picture going that bit more special, as was the film.

Arriving for work

Boilers and clinkers.

During these first few months I had made friends with the Chief Projectionist at the other cinema in town, the Odeon. It turned out that Frank used to be a projectionist at the Abbeygate before moving on and I spent quite a lot of my free time either visiting his projection room or just watching their film show. It was also about this time I ventured further afield and payed a return visit to Geoff High, who had recently popped in for a visit.

This was another small independent cinema in Thetford that mixed its time with cinema and bingo. I took an instant liking to Geoff as he reminded me somewhat of Len and the cinema, 'The Palace' was very akin to the old New England, a truly one-man band. I used to enjoy my visits there, listening to his stories of years gone past. His projection equipment was new to me, BTH and it was a challenge to learn about something different. I would often run a few reels whilst he was off attending to something downstairs. I was a frequent visitor there up until its closure to become a full time bingo hall.

Then that fateful day arrived for me to re-take my motor cycle driving test. I hadn't a clue where I was going, round all these back streets. I even had to weave my way through what seemed like a churchyard with gravestones either side. It was quite off putting, when suddenly this examiner jumped out from behind one of the grave stones. Talk about 'Emergency stop!' I nearly messed myself, but by some quirk of fate at the end of this ordeal I had done enough to get a pass.

Life was seemingly good to me. I was enjoying my work and all the newfound friends along the way. I would go home every few weeks, sometimes for a weekend.

It was on one of these weekends, I had the urge to look in at the New England and see how it was doing, but I wished afterwards I hadn't. The entire place looked a shambles and the unknown person in the projection room didn't seem to care less, and didn't give me the time of day. I just had a swift look round. Mr Alderman was not there so I had a quick glance at 'Von Ryan's Express' and took my leave. Five weeks later I heard that the cinema had closed.

CHAPTER 11

As the year passed by I learnt so much, mostly from things that had broken down and from working closely with the Westrex projection engineer, Stan Boxshall, whom I would become great friends with over the years. He would periodically service our equipment.

We now had a trainee projectionist on the staff, usually a sixteen year old and a first taste of full time employment. We went through several of these as not everyone could get used to working evenings and weekends and of course the income was very minimal.

After a while some jobs could get delegated like the boiler and film rewinding. The day I was showing '2001 A Space Odyssey', this film had the compulsory intermission. After the allocated time we started up the second half and to my shock and horror only one half of the curtains opened. I rushed from the projection room down to the screen end and found the cable had snapped. Luckily we kept a two-stage ladder behind the proscenium. It meant climbing this ladder in pitch darkness and crawling along the top of the screen frame, some thirty feet up, and manually pushing open the half curtain. The film was still showing and it seemed very unreal to have HAL, the talking computer directly below you singing "Daisy Daisy".

Still, I got the Job accomplished; the cable repair could wait until the morning.

I was showing the matinee performance of 'Half A Sixpence' one day when suddenly, without warning the cry went up "No Sound". As the duty projectionist the onus is on you, but amplifiers are not my forte. I had no choice but to stop the film and start checking the obvious reasons. All these checks failed to turn up anything. I next had to take the covers off the amplifier, Kalee Duosonic, noting how long we had been off screen. You could just faintly hear the noise from the auditorium and the house phone was ringing off the wall. "What should we tell the patrons?" I didn't know yet. Panic setting in, I went back to the amplifier. Two rows of valves and a multitude of resistors and coils. It could be anything. I raced to the spares cabinet and started changing the valves in turn. With five changed there was still no sound and we had been over ten minutes off screen now and I was no further forward. I was thinking about giving up now and calling the engineer, 'the specialist'. There were two big grey valves, KT66 stamped on them. 'Have we got any spares?' Yes, one at the very back of the cabinet. I pulled out the first one with great difficulty and burnt two fingers in the process, put the new one in but there was no joy. Feeling completely useless now I tugged the other one out in sheer frustration and as I did, there was a loud crack across the speaker that made me jump out of my skin. I placed the other used one in the amplifier and it came back to life. We were off again. What a day.

All the different pieces of equipment working in harmony together to give a perfect performance. It only took one hiccup to upset the routine and it's only when things go wrong that the projectionist gets noticed. The amount of times I had, after telling someone that I worked at the cinema, I would be told, "I went to see a film there and it broke down." No one ever says what a good show it was.

The year 1966 was passing by at a rate and we installed a small black & white television set in our rest room so that we could see the World cup final. As I wasn't into football at that time I concentrated on the projection of Paul Newman in 'The Drowning Pool' and let the others watch it, I do remember flashing the final score on the screen by way of a hand written message on the slide lantern.

It was a few months later that Doug told me he had invited the young girl, who had moved into one of the flats with her mother, to come down and watch a film.

I had noticed her through their kitchen window which overlooked the entrance to the projection room. I knew she was about my age and had long hair, so as to make a good impression I popped home during my tea break and dressed for the occasion.

At 7.30 p.m. she duly arrived and Doug showed her in and did the introductions to this very shy person who had previously no experience with young girls, then he settled her on the high stool looking out of the observation port to watch the film 'The Man from Uncle'. All I could do was to keep peeping through the projectors at her and get a smile each time I went to rewind a reel of film.

The evening passed by so quickly and she was gone. I spent the next few weeks glancing up at her window in the hopes of seeing her again, then one day it just happened and I got a wave for my troubles.

Could I pluck up the courage to ask her out? I had seen it done a thousand times on screen, but all I got was a cold sweat. Then the inevitable happened.

I bumped into her, quite by accident. She was coming up the flat stairway as I was going down, it was too good an opportunity to miss and after the initial hello's I just blurted it out. Would she like to come out with me on my next evening off? To my astonishment, she said "Yes. Let me know when." All that worrying for nothing.

My next evening off was soon upon me and I was at the pre-arranged meeting place for seven o'clock. It turned out that her mother had forbidden her to go out on a date, so in order to get away she was "baby sitting" and had to be back in by ten. I could handle that, but where were we to go? I hadn't given any thought to that and at seven o'clock just about everywhere was closed. We ended up in a Chinese restaurant having sausage egg and chips and a fit of the giggles. Not very oriental! We talked none stop all evening and really hit it off. Not wanting to rock the boat, we parted company at ten on the dot, with a peck on the cheek, and I floated home on cloud nine.

Over the next few weeks films took second place in my mind, perhaps with the exception of 'In The Heat of the Night' and 'Rosemary's Baby'. I always seemed to be clock watching for the pre-ordained time when the kitchen window would open and we could have a chat, interrupted by me rushing off to do a reel change. Apart from our first evening out and due to her mother's domineering attitude that she should not fraternise with the likes of me, it was going to be difficult to get out together again.

It was now December and this was to be the first Christmas I would spend away from home. I had written several letters home telling my parents all about this girl I'd met and the problems that ensued. They always wrote back full of encouragement and seemed genuinely happy for me. They said "bring her home with you whenever you want". Bring her home? I couldn't even get her out.

Our next encounter was a chat through Doug's kitchen window, which was on the same level as the projection room, just outside our second exit and we would often be popping out to collect something from his kitchen. It was no surprise when he sent me there to collect a cuppa for us both, but to my surprise the person the other side of the window was Geraldine who had been paying a planned visit. This would be our closest encounter since our night out together. Luckily I had in our rest room a card and present waiting for her. I had been hoping for just such a moment. During the course of our meeting I ran back in so as to be able to wish her a happy Christmas and with my Christmas card and present clutched in her hand we said our goodnights. It was then a case of back to the old routine of catching a glimpse, whenever.

I spent Christmas Day with Bill and Margaret. It was a quiet affair and my mind wasn't really with it. I was constantly wondering whether she had liked the makeup compact (Marie's suggestion). I was just waiting for Boxing Day to come round so as to get back to work.

It duly did and there was my girl at the window all waves and smiles, the world suddenly seemed a lot brighter.

Doug and his wife Marie knew of our plight and came to the rescue by inviting Geraldine to a New Year's Eve dance with them at the British Legion Club. I was to join them at the end of the show. This ruse worked a treat and on the due date, funnily enough, the show finished a little bit earlier that night and I was running up the road to the British Legion to join the party.

And what a night we had. I certainly didn't want it to finish but alas we were back at Doug and Marie's flat having a coffee between our mad passionate embraces. We had waited a long time for this moment and to let each other know our true feelings, and we weren't going to waste it. We only had eyes for each other that night, but it was suddenly two o'clock in the morning and she had to go.

Oh what a party we had.

We said our goodnights with heavy hearts, wondering when the next time of togetherness would be.

Two days later, working away in the projection room, a loud knocking at the rear door shattered the peace. Upon opening our door a complete stranger stood there and introduced himself as Geraldine's brother. He had come to warn me not to continue seeing his sister. To say I was taken aback was an understatement, as he followed me inside ranting about the right and wrongs of a young relationship and the fact that his mother needed her and it would not be in my interests to get involved. Suddenly Doug stepped into the fray and sent me down to the projector end to complete a change over. I could hear him calming the situation, and saying why don't you leave them alone, I also heard the reply that he had to do this, but didn't want to. They were moving out of the flat so there was no point in it any longer. With that he left and the rest of the evening seemed to merge into a mind twisting mist. (some forty years later we have been re-acquainted and become two proper brothers-in-law, funny old world)

A couple of days went by and try as I may, I could not seem to be in the right place, at the right time to meet my girl as she came in from work. Then this one particular evening, there she was. She stood at the projection room door looking drawn and pale. I was working with Doug and he motioned that I should go into the rest room with her and a cup of tea was the course of action. It seemed that her mother had guessed all along about our New Year rendezvous and had called her deceitful and forbidden her to leave the flat except for work.

Between the sobs of distress I understood that her mother had decided to move back into the house she shared with her son and daughter-in-law. I in some small way felt guilty in causing some of her distress. When she told me she would have no choice but to go with her mother, there and then I decided (against all advice) to go up to the flat and confront her mother. Instantly, or so it seemed I was knocking on her door and went in. She rounded on me with a tirade of insults. I couldn't get a word in edgeways. There was no reasoning and within no time at all she had, after taking a wild swipe at me, grabbed her coat and rushed off to her son. I made my way back to break the news of the events and formulate plans, when suddenly the sister-in law put in an appearance and, surprise surprise, was in agreement to helping us in our plight. It seemed that the mother ranted herself into a state of disowning her only daughter in exactly the same way she had done when the brother had wanted to get married. She had now shut herself into a room and wouldn't see anyone. So what to do? We sat all night in the dark cold kitchen of that ill-fated flat, a bit bewildered but in reality, with only two choices, move back home and give up our feelings for each other, (not really an option) or find somewhere for her to live. We would scour the local papers in the morning.

Next day she rang into 'The Hand Laundry' where she worked as a seamstress and arranged the morning off. Then, as if fate had shown a hand, there in the paper was an advert for a single room, bed-sit, ideal for a young female. It was also in the near vicinity. We hurried round and after an interview with a charming old lady, the deal was done. She had three single bed-sit rooms in this house, all occupied with ladies. After a quick inspection of the room, which consisted of a single bed, dresser, sideboard, chair and table, gas fire and a single gas ring, it seemed to be the answer to our prayers. We both went back to work that afternoon feeling very content, even with the no male visitors rule.

Getting settled in

Snug as a bug comes to mind!

I spent the afternoon writing home to my parents outlining all the previous events and promising to bring her home as soon as possible.

It was to be her 21st birthday at the end of the month and I had the weekend off, so it could be then.

The next few weeks settled down into a round of work, followed by long hours pressed together against the January cold outside her bed-sit, before saying our goodnights and making my way back to my lodgings. My evenings off were spent together in either the Odeon or the back row of the Abbeygate. I felt comfortable in the surroundings of a cinema, my second home, and it was the one place we could be together. Despite the invitations to visit different people, which we did gratefully get round to most of them, but just holding hands watching 'The Blue Max', 'Peyton Place', 'Magnificent Men in Their Flying Machines', and many others was more than idyllic to me.

It was now all arranged that the last weekend of the month we would be going home for her to meet my family and to spend her 21st birthday there. I knew this was a daunting thought for her, not only meeting my parents but having to travel such a distance on the back of my motor bike, and what would she look like when we arrived?

During the prior week she received a letter from my mother saying how they were all looking forward to meeting her and to wrap up warm on that old bike, it wasn't going to be a fashion parade, just get there safe. That did the trick and seemed to allay any underlying fears.

Friday evening the 26th January 1967 and we were off, cruising the A45 at 50 miles an hour with my girl hanging on for grim death, the weather was kind to us. It was a dry crisp evening, and we went straight through without a stop and duly arrived in Ramsey at 8.30 p.m. As I was pushing the bike up our garden path the front door opened and light spilled out, immediately followed with every family member. They went straight past me and with arms outstretched guided Geraldine into the warmth of the house. I don't think anyone stopped talking for the rest of the night. I know my father was fascinated with her Suffolk accent and from that moment on she had become part of the family. I do think she was a little overwhelmed with it all and not used to being the centre of attention. It must have seemed strange having a father figure looking over her, as sadly she had never known her own father. He had died whilst undergoing surgery when she was only six weeks old.

The weekend was a complete success culminating on the Sunday with a 21st Birthday spread. Everything seemed so fitting just like a jigsaw puzzle, when all the pieces suddenly slot into shape.

Daredevil days

A party to remember for always

We got there OK. What a happy weekend we had

But all too soon it was time for us to depart and with our suitcase now in a bulging state firmly tied on to the Carrier, we said our goodbyes and proceeded Back to Bury St Edmunds. A journey we would be making on numerous occasions over the years to come.

Back to the reality of work, our latest young trainee Trevor Baker was to leave at the end of the week, just when he was becoming useful so all the little delegated menial jobs would have to be done by yours truly again, no more perks of delegating for a while.

CHAPTER 12

During the next few weeks life took on a regular pattern of her slipping up the back staircase after work and spending the evening with me in the projection room, or sitting writing letters in our little rest room.

After the show we would stroll back to her digs and huddle together on the doorstep for hours before having to part company and go our separate ways. I would be creeping in my lodgings in the small wee hours trying not to disturb anyone, only to be told next morning, "You were late again last night."

At the cinema we had taken on yet another school leaver as a trainee projectionist. Eddie was a little different from some of the others before him and we instantly bonded. He was like a younger brother and it made our training sessions good fun sometimes to the bemusement of Douggie who was also now deputising as a manager during busy periods and Mr Berry's days off. Our shifts seemed to run opposite for most weeks.

It was during this time that a film production crew partly took over the Angel Hotel at the rear of the cinema and approached the management regarding the hiring of the cinema (after our normal shows) for the purpose of screening the previous days 'rushes'. This was well before the advent of instant photography and video. The day's filming was rushed to the film laboratories in London, processed and rushed back for viewing by the film crew with special scrutiny by the Director and Chief Camera man (John Coquillon), who liked to view from the projection room. He was a real nice guy. The film was 'The Witchfinder General' and had many location shots and purposefully built film sets all around Suffolk.

VINCENT PRICE

IAN OGILVY **RUPERT DAVIES**

WITCHFINDER GENERAL

As the time approached for the first session of these experiences, we didn't really know what to expect and was told the film they wanted to see would come with them. We waited for what seemed like an eternity, staring out of the portholes, waiting for the film crew to arrive. Suddenly the bottom exit doors opened and in flowed about thirty people all with glasses in hand. It seemed they had all come from the Hotel bar straight to our nearest door and were having a high old time, then as if right on cue, the chief cameraman and his assistant came in with an armful of film tins and proceeded to tell us in what order they wanted to view them. Being new film stock we had to don these white cotton gloves in order to handle the stock without any finger marks. We proceeded to splice on our leaders and make ready for projecting. Each tin contained approximately one or two minutes of film. With everyone ready, off we went. The very first image on screen was the clapperboard and it was noticed that the assistant cameraman was furiously scribbling down notes as each scene seemed to be repeated at different angles. With that reel over, we started the next one off. John Coquillon was intently staring out of the projector port when he suddenly shouted out and frightened the life out me, "Bugger it, I missed him completely." It turned out the hero was galloping through the woods and the camera only picked out the moving branches not the rider. There was a re-shoot the next day, but I always think of that moment whenever I see the film.

The evenings became the highlight of our days and gave us a completely different insight from Exhibiting to film making. It became the same ritual each night. A procession from the hotel bar into the cinema to see yesterday's filming. Then one night in strolled Vincent Price, the star of the film, to see his sequences. WOW!

I had shown most of his films through the years and to see him in the cinema was something else.

The weeks passed by and soon this saga came to an end. On the final evening of showing the daily rushes we all got invited back to the hotel to join the 'end of shoot' party. It was at this time I found myself chatting away to Rupert Davis, star of the television series *Maigret*. I even got his autograph, I would be watching out for this film which I was told would be out next year.

It was now coming up to Easter and I had known my girl for about four months and we both felt the same way, even more so after breaking the No Male Visitor rule, well it was cold outside!

I do believe we mutually agreed that the next step was to get engaged. Well, why not? They do it in the films all the time. I know she was looking in all the jeweller's windows at every opportunity. Eventually the ring was spotted and the deposit paid. It was decided that on my next day off we would collect the ring and go to Ipswich and see 'The Sound of Music' at the Gaumont to celebrate the occasion. The day went like clockwork, we became officially engaged, and Edelweiss became 'our song' in memory of the day.

The Happiest Sound In All The World
Christopher Plummer & Julie Andrews

THE SOUND OF MUSIC

We still get romantic over this film.

We went home to Ramsey to share the news with them on Easter Sunday. Everyone was so happy, it was the right and proper thing to do. Soon after, and just as if fate had taken a helping hand, Geraldine, my girl came rushing home from work in a state of high excitement. It turned out that at the rear of the Hand Laundry where she worked, there was an area which had these war-time Nissan huts. Five of them, in which employees of the laundry would rent out for accommodation. Two were unused, had been for a long while but would I like to have a look? Off we went, not quite sure what to expect.

The keys had been left with one of the tenants. She obviously knew them all as laundry employees and I felt like the odd one out, but at least they didn't crowd us, just gave us the keys and let us get on with it. To say these units were neglected was an understatement. One was a complete wooden structure, raised off the ground and had a railed veranda. Inside it was and smelt so damp and fusty we both said let's look at the other one.

We walked up to the front door 'Glendale'. This plaque had been put on years ago, but it still had a ring to it. Once inside, we noted how cold it was, but not too damp. A long narrow hall ran the length of the building with a door at the end of it. Working from the front door, there was a toilet to the left then working up the passage, a reasonably large room which would make a bedroom. Next another room, similar in size, another bedroom or living room, then the door at the end led into the kitchenette. There was also a coal fireplace in this room. It seemed as if this room had been converted at some stage to incorporate a bathroom which was built into the corner. It was just big enough for a bath, with an emersion heater fixed to the wall above it and a small hand basin with just a cold water tap. That was about it.

We both thought, that if anything, this was the one we could make habitable with a bit of work, so the very next day she signed up an employee's rent agreement for 'Glendale' at the bargain rate of ten shillings per week. I don't think we stopped talking about it all night it was to be our castle. On my next day off we arranged to have the electricity connected and I balanced a sack of coal from the garage on my motorbike. We lit the fire just to air the rooms out then, as if by magic a knock on the door and there was this two-seater settee and a chair. Would we like it? It's being thrown away! That was Johnny, our new neighbour. Soon after that another knock, Fred and Irene. "We have an old bed going spare would you like it?"

We spent the whole night huddled up on that settee in the firelight of our first home together.

As the weeks passed it seemed everyone we knew wanted to share our good fortune and give us something for our new home.

Back way into Glendale

Decorating our first home together

Getting our new home habitable.

Just moved in all re-decorated

Chuffed with my cooking attempt.

Kitchen all finished

Back at the cinema we were having a change of projection equipment due to our sister cinema in Dereham closing down and the projectors there were better than ours. They were to be shipped over and installed with us. The object was to re-build these two projectors in the spare space in the rewind area so they could be well tested. Then on the appointed night they were moved into position. After the dismantling of the ones in use, it turned out to be the usual Independent DIY installation; odd bits of projector would keep coming over in the back of someone's car and would have to be stored away until it was needed. This seemed to go on for weeks before we got down to the task of re-building them. Our regular service Engineer Stan Boxshall worked for the Westrex Company who supplied sound and projection equipment to the cinema industry. He was assigned to oversee the installation and ensure the sound and picture was fully operational.

The appointed night soon came round and after the show we set to the task of dismantling and removing the two projectors that had served us well but were now floundering.

It took several hours to dismantle two projectors, putting aside the parts we would need again and being sure not to damage any cable ends. Assembling a projector then moving it across a room and into place is much better in theory than in practice. We all hugged and heaved to make the thing move, tearing up some floor tiles in the process. There was another one to do after this.

By six o'clock in the morning, we were all now a bit weary, but were nearly ready for a film test. As I threaded up a reel of 'The Long, The Short and The Tall',

The tragic story of seven British soldiers trapped behind Japanese lines. There can be no second chances

THE LONG AND THE SHORT AND THE TALL

we started the first test. Whoops! The bottom spool wasn't going round so we had to stop in a hurry. The film was piling onto the floor. We found the cause. The clutch was slipping. The take-up spool was belt driven with a slip clutch that would take the pressure of a reel of film without losing the tension required to keep up with the projector speed. Two leather discs rubbed together with a spring loaded tension clamp. It most likely got some oil on during the re-construction of the projector and was slipping. We cleaned up the discs, roughened with sandpaper and then off we went again. Laurence Harvey doing his bit in the Burmese jungle and with just a few minor adjustments number one projector was ready to roll.

It was a different story with the other one. The on screen image was ghosting badly, that's when the light shutter and intermittent sprocket are out of sync. It's a partial strip down to get at the parts required to remedy the fault.

After several attempts we succeeded and all was well, but hang on a minute there was no sound, just a high-pitched hum. This is where Stan, the Westrex man really came into play. Amplifiers have always been a mystery to me, valves, cathodes, diodes resistors and such like. Some things are left well alone whilst they work, but this morning was a different story. A process of elimination ensued until all was well and we had identical picture quality from each projector. It was now ten o'clock and mission accomplished. It was decided that we would go home catch a couple of hours sleep and be ready for the two o'clock matinee. That would be the real tester, but we need not have worried. The night's work having gone to plan, gave us a trouble-free show the next day.

Cheers! Our new, second hand projectors in the background

CHAPTER 13

Life had started to settle down and it seemed the obvious thing to do was the getting married bit.; We had spoken of it in passing but not set any dates. Don't ask me why but I said October most likely just for the sake of seeming positive, so that was that then. I was happily in my projection room projecting illusions onto the screen whilst plans were being formulated and I was amazed just how many people wanted to be involved.

I only had one reservation and that was not having the other mother involved and after several discussions on the subject, I persuaded Geraldine to go and see her, if only to say we would be doing this with or without her blessing. With her sister-in-law's help, a visit was made. I opted to keep out of the way so as not to antagonise the situation, but just as her brother experienced, all turned out well and there was great relief all round.

Upon reflection it was the right decision for me not to be there as I was never blessed with too much patience, and I was better served showing Cornel Wilde in 'The Naked Prey' whilst this fragile re-union was going on.

From then on we forged ahead with renewed vigour. A church; reception venue; photographer; the list seemed endless. We had to meet the vicar that was a laugh, he gave us a pep talk, but he was really nice. However I was informed that as I was only twenty we would have to ask my parents to fill in a consent form for him to proceed. Good job it wasn't the other way around. Roll on October – I'd be a nervous wreck before then. Every spare moment away from the sanctuary of the projection room was taken up with wedding preparations and listening intently at all the well-meaning advice. Money was in short supply as a projectionist was not the best paid job going, that's how the phrase "they do it for the love of the job" comes to mind, which meant budgeting was paramount and we spent our evenings together at 'Glendale' formulating plans. The wedding date was now firmly set for Saturday 28th October 1967 and we could now start to plan ahead. A couple of years earlier I had been Best Man at my brother Pete's wedding and was always expecting him to do the same for me, only to be told that he would be unable to attend as his baby should be arriving the very same weekend, and the journey from Plymouth was out of the question. What a bummer, but as luck would have it I had gotten to know Geraldine's best friend Marilyn and her boyfriend David quite well and it seemed an obvious choice to ask him to be my best man. After a slight nervous hesitation it was agreed and another obstacle had been overcome. I could now get back to the projection room without that worry and it was Christopher Lee doing his Dracula impersonation as 'The Prince of Darkness' I used to love these type of films and would stand by the sound control just to give that extra surge of volume so as to watch the audience below jump out of their seats, as it was most often the sudden noise, not the scene that made them jump.

On our next visit home my parents announced that they would very much like to supply the material and make our bridesmaid dresses. I have to freely admit that I kept a low profile so as not to offend anyone, as it seemed everyone wanted to be involved.

Perhaps they couldn't believe I would actually go through with it as I spent the weekend telling my father about Steve McQueen in 'Bullet'., Whilst this was going on the girls had decided that four bridesmaids would be the correct balance two from each family, well I wasn't going to argue. The next two months just flashed by and it was October and the jitters started to set in I don't think I was much use to anyone, although I did spend my evenings off making invitation cards, then back to the sanctuary of the projection room to get lost in my film world.

October 22nd my two weeks' holiday started a week prior for preparations and a week after to wind down. As we couldn't afford a honeymoon away we were to spend the week at my parents so that we could visit my friends and relations in Peterborough, but that was to be after one of the most hectic weeks I had ever experienced.

The week was spent racing in ever decreasing circles between all the different friends that were playing a part in our preparations. At work we had just started a two week run of this highly acclaimed film (that alone made it extra special) it was Warren Beatty and Faye Dunaway in 'Bonnie and Clyde' and as my own life events seemed to be overtaking me I longed to be back in the projection room if only to re-group my thoughts, but the Friday night soon came round and I was to stay with my best man David at his home for the night and Geraldine would be at Glendale with Marilyn. The next time we would meet would be in the Congregational church at two o'clock. David lived just outside Bury and as it was late at night I had no idea where I was and spent most of the night lying awake wondering what lay ahead. It seemed a great relief when it was finally time to get up go downstairs and chat with David's parents who I only knew briefly beforehand and whilst he had a 'lie in' I went for a stroll along the country lanes adjacent to the cottage to gather my thoughts of what lay ahead. It was another of those bright cloudless mornings and by the time I got back feeling quite refreshed from the time alone David was up and about and in no time at all it was time to get ready for the main event. We arrived back in Bury in plenty of time; our due arrival time at the church was to be 1.45 p.m. so it was a stop off at the Queens Head for a drop of 'Dutch courage' and by the time we took our leave to head for the church we first noticed how overcast the sky had become." Hope it doesn't rain" I heard David say, but I was getting to grips with my thoughts after that drink and must say felt a bit tipsy to say the least. Once at the church the Reverend Ivory met us at the door and just ran through the procedure once again, but it was more the case of acknowledging the waves of family members and friends. Once in position it was just a matter of waiting for the bride, and trying not to get a fit of the 'giggles.' After what seemed like an eternity the wedding march burst forth and in she walked I turned to get a look and what a surprise. I hadn't seen her wedding dress before and with her hair fastened up and the face veiled she looked quite tall walking down that aisle on the arm of her brother. As we came together I was at a complete loss for words and just said, "You are late." To which she whispered, "We haven't got a barman." Never mind, on with the show.

The service went off very well, just some giggles on my part, a drink and a few nerves was all it took. I did notice that it had started to rain and thought I hoped it wouldn't spoil the photograph session that was to come. After the customary signing of the register we led the congregation outside and our luck was holding the rain had stopped, cameras and confetti suddenly took over, then into the car for the short drive to the reception. Most of our guests just walked the short distance, and upon arrival our closest friends were busy scurrying around getting drinks poured before the bulk of guests arrived. The only glitch was as Geraldine had said – the person who was going to be barman wasn't well and couldn't be with us, never mind, our neighbour Fred stepped into the breach and saved the day.

Only one problem no one could find a bottle opener. Once everyone was settled I gathered up a few bottles and some eat-treats and slipped off to the cinema, which wasn't far away.

The look of shock and horror on their faces when I walked into the projection room was a picture, "Just brought you both a drink seeing's that you can't be with us. "Oh yes, it will cost the loan of a bottle opener."

After a quick look at Faye Dunaway and Warren Beatty doing their 'Bonnie and Clyde' routine I took my leave,

WARREN BEATTY FAYE DUNAWAY

They're young . . .
they're in love
and they kill people

BONNIE AND CLYDE

and as I made my way back to the reception the heavens opened, thunder, lightning, the lot. I ran down the street thinking how lucky we were that this didn't arrive an hour earlier. At the end of the evening a ride home to Ramsey had been arranged in a friend of Mum and Dad's car, "not having you both arrive on a motorbike" they said in unison; "we have made up a bed in the front room that is your room for the week, nudge nudge wink wink". Why do they always do that? And the crème de la crème statement, "You know what tonight is, the clocks go back, you will have an extra hour!" Hilarious laughter all round, but not from me.

David and Me after a drop of Dutch courage; meet the missus

Trying to be serious; anyone for cake

Family shot with the in-laws, bridesmaids; two from each family

The so called 'Honeymoon Week' flashed by, what with so many people to visit and soon it was time to go back to Bury. Their friend Dave, with whom Dad worked with at the local RAF Camp in Upwood, had volunteered to do a return visit for us and Mum and Dad came along for the ride, and they all safely deposited us in our new abode as Mr and Mrs. The very next day, Sunday, I was back at work just trying to settle back into the routine. The days suddenly seemed to drag, which was a new experience for me, and as we now didn't see each other during the working day, only after I got in late each night, it was a strain. I felt it more as some weeks I would only have one weekday off then she would be working and that's how the weeks passed by, although she never once complained, when we had to constantly turn down invitations to go out with friends, it was just me that felt awkward.

We had our first Christmas together in our own home; another milestone, but I could feel myself becoming increasingly restless at work. The pay structure had not altered, and we were struggling as our first set of bills came in, this went on for several months and I felt we were existing, not living. Then on one of our few weekends home to Ramsey the journey back was the most horrendous.

A gale blew up from nowhere and my poor old motorbike just couldn't cope with a head on wind and the lashing rain and we limped back into Bury three hours later having pushed it the last few miles. I promised that she would never have to ride on it again.

It was now coming up to my 21st birthday and during a break from showing 'The Dirty Dozen' I found myself knocking on the manager's door; upon entering I think he sensed something was on my mind and invited me to talk over any problems I had. Upon reflection, him being a confirmed bachelor he just couldn't grasp how I felt about not being able to provide for my new circumstances, but we parted with the promise he would discuss it with the owner. I went home that night feeling much relieved and over the next week showing films seemed a much better prospect. The Friday came round and as usual we went to the office to collect our weekly pay. As I stood there waiting to sign for mine I got a big grin and a – "Who's a lucky boy then?" I was to be given an extra ten shillings per week. I walked out dumfounded that they thought this was my worth. My first pay rise for two years and yet it remained pounds under the lowest 'married man's' wage. I went back up into the projection room and immediately wrote out a week's notice and marched back into the office and presented it to a bewildered management who considered me to be so very ungrateful.

That night back at home I explained my reasons to the shell-shocked wife who's only reaction was that I should go straight back and tell them it was a mistake. She was adamant we would manage on our pooled resources, but to me it was a matter of pride and I was looking for another job. During the next week it was certainly a mixed atmosphere at work; Doug was imploring me not to leave, but the manager was still under the impression I had been disrespectful to their generous offer.

On my day off that week I had secured a job at a printing firm Lamson & Paragon as a general labourer starting at eight o'clock Monday morning, with a wage of over double what I was getting (even with the extra ten shillings). Alas the week came to an end and so did my job as a projectionist.

CHAPTER 14

Monday morning and as I made my way into this new world of regimented procedures, union rules, and the noise of printing presses, I just stood there looked around and thought, “What have I done.” After a few weeks of this despite the extra income life at home had suddenly become very tetchy, I knew it was me; I missed my films and all these evenings at home when I should have been showing them hung heavy on my conscience.

Within two months we had saved up a deposit for some new transport and I had decided that as I only had a motor bike licence we would get one of those three wheeler reliant cars. I could drive one of those and we could go home again; we hadn’t been since that fateful night of the gales, so that was the plan.

Easter 1968 over to Revets of Stowmarket and chose a blue Reliant. I paid the deposit plus a part exchange of my old bike and was told I could pick it up in three days’ time. I suddenly felt apprehensive because I had never driven a car before and whilst it may have been legal to have a three wheeler, it was still car size and that worried me.

On the pick-up day luckily our friends Billy and Sheila came with us and he drove me to a remote spot for some practice before letting me loose on the roads. The very next morning, Easter Sunday, I was off out to the shop in my new car feeling as proud as a peacock when suddenly at the end of the road there was a very sharp bend with a policeman directing the traffic for an Easter parade. I was going much too fast to make the bend, steering wheel hard down and over we went with my new car scraping across the road, then whack as it hit the curb it miraculously bounced up onto its three wheels and came to a stop right at the foot of that policeman.

Talk about ‘Pride before a fall,’ my world had just come crashing down. After having all my particulars taken down, as they say, I then had to go home and show everyone my handiwork.

I didn’t venture back out on the road for over a week, still feeling very embarrassed I couldn’t face going back to Revets to get my car mended so I went to Millwards in Newmarket and all went well from then on.

I had been away from cinema life for nearly three months now and the yearning within me to show another film was stronger than ever.

I tolerated my job at the printers, but only because I had to and it wasn't worth changing it. One would be as bad as another. Evenings at home had become torture, between seven and ten o'clock I just felt lost, as this is when I should have been screening the day's busy performance, and I was stuck here.

A few days later I bumped into Douggie and he asked why I never went up to see him, I don't think he really understood that I just could not bring myself to go into the projection room and not be part of it. He finished by saying that they couldn't find another projectionist and would I like to do a bit of part-time work so he could have a break as he was moving out of the cinema flat into a house on one of the estates.

I said I would think it over, but I raced home with heart pounding to tell the news only to hear, "Can't you go full time?"

So the very next evening I was back in the projection room. It was like I had never been away; the film wasn't very memorable, Burt Lancaster in 'The Swimmer'. I spent the next five evenings working in my element without pay for three of them as that was my choice, but I didn't care, I was back where I belonged. One evening during the very next week I was asked down to the manager's office and there sat the owner Mr Miller, "What's all this silliness? Let's see if we can make amends." After a while a new weekly wage was agreed. I know it was a third less than I was now earning elsewhere, but it didn't seem to matter and the deal was done. I would re-start back full time the very next week, and wow! The film was to be 'The Witchfinder General'. I just had to be there for that. I told anyone who would listen that I would be re-turning to the cinema full time, even the people I worked with at the printers and just about everyone said the same thing, "About time too" or words to that effect.

I was back and revelling in it. 'The Witchfinder General' brought back so many good memories. It seemed strange seeing the final version after so many takes when screening 'the rushes' for the film crew. The next few weeks and then months just seemed to fly by. Home life was total bliss again, we had our little three-wheeler so I could pop off home whatever the weather, but as it always seems nothing lasts for long. I knew that Douggie was spending more and more time downstairs even when he was not deputising for the manager, he was having a dalliance with one of the usherettes, I don't think it was anything serious, just a bit of infatuation, but I was called into the office one night and asked outright if it came to a head would I take over as chief projectionist, well of course I said yes and that seemed to put a pre-planned series of events into place, plans that I had no prior knowledge o., Poor old Douggie, I'm sure he thought that I had grassed him up to get his job. I suppose on reflection I would have thought the same because at the end of the show the very next Saturday night he was paid off and I became Chief. On the odd occasions we met after that he was always very cool, I suppose someone had to take the blame. For me a new chapter in my life was just beginning.

CHAPTER 15

The very first hurdle was to find an assistant, so the adverts went out in the trade press as well as the local papers. It's a funny old business and these adverts seem to bring out all the oddballs who have ever had any association within the cinema industry or beyond, like the enthusiastic amateur who has dabbled with some 8mm home movie film and needs a job to see him through till the building trade picked up or the 60-year-old army veteran who showed a film from the back of a lorry in the North African desert campaign; the list was endless.

It was a shame that my trainee 'Eddie' was not yet ready to take the next step. During the many interviews I did as chief it amazed me just how many applicants had no idea just what goes on in a projection room, 'we just sit and watch films all day.'

After a couple of weeks of this charade a pleasant young man came in response to our advert, it turned out he wanted to move back to this area, his home being in the village of Woolpit., and he was currently working in a cinema at Hastings. We instantly hit it off, so with myself, David and Eddie, the team was complete and work settled down very nicely, we were all getting regular days off and on our full days on together we would have a one hour Tea break away from site, David who had become attached to one of the usherettes would jump on his moped and spend the hour when she was not working at her home just outside Bury, young Eddie would either go for a stroll round the town or downstairs to watch an hour of film depending on the weather, me I would pop home and use up my hour in a domestic way.

Then came the fateful night that David did not return from his break and as the evening passed by with no news of his whereabouts rumours were running rife. Then at ten o'clock a family member rang in to tell us that David had been in a terrible accident on his moped and had subsequently died from his injuries. The news left us rather shell-shocked to say the least and at the end of the show Eddie and myself made our way home to 'Glendale' where we spent the night mourning the passing of our colleague.

The following weeks passed by slowly and with only a trainee it meant I had worked now for four weeks solid and was in need of a day off. Legally no one under the age of eighteen could be left in charge of a projection room, so that ruled out Eddie in any imagination. During the next year or so we had a succession of short term projectionists all of different calibres, but at least it meant some time off and domestic bliss, not that any pressure was ever put upon me to be at home, having experienced my time away from the cinema neither of us wanted a repeat performance.

Then out of the blue Mr Berry informed me that David's younger brother had applied for his job albeit he had some limited experience in projection but due to the circumstances Mr Berry thought he was doing us all a favour in starting him on without any prior consultation or introductions, and the deed was done. The very next week on his start day we were all on duty as a sort of 'get to know you' shift, it was hard work to say the least, not all his fault I think he just kept bringing back the memories we had of his brother and as he was such an opposite it made it doubly hard.

Working life settled down and at least I was getting some time off, which proved very useful as the local council had approached the landlord of the dwellings we lived in – 'Glendale' being one of them – and told him that to continue renting out the properties a modernisation programme would have to be put into place. To the Landlord this was not a viable option so we were to be re-housed into a council house on one of the estates, after 18 months of sheer bliss in our castle the thought of moving away was tinged with sadness, but we both knew it couldn't go on forever, we had to move forward.

The day soon seemed to be upon us and we were transporting our belongings into a two bedroomed council house, it was certainly a modern outlook after the rear of the Hand Laundry, but I never felt settled there, in fact just the opposite, money was now tight, the rent was five times higher than 'Glendale' and the in-laws all lived in the near vicinity. Geraldine didn't have a problem with this in fact she seemed quite happy with her lot being able to visit on a regular basis. Her mother who was living in a flat of her own just down the hill, was by now well and truly back in her life, and in my mind was ruling our lives. I had noticed that she would be frantically just getting in before my workday was over and on the occasions she never made it in time arguments would pursue, it just couldn't go on. My brother / sister-in-law who were only a few streets away didn't help the situation and I began to feel trapped by it all. By now we had an addition to the family by way of our Golden Labrador 'Jason' (named after the film 'Jason and the Argonauts') and you would often find me over the fields with him on my off time, Geraldine had by now left the Hand Laundry and was about to do some part-time usherette work at the cinema, that would be nice and at least help the household budget with which we were struggling on with just a projectionist wage. Cinema business was in the doldrums so the struggle for survival seemed all around us.

By this time I had sold my Reliant back to the dealership, as I just couldn't afford to keep up the repayments, so no transport now just a trusty old cycle. Christmas 1970 was to be another milestone in my life, we had been invited to have Christmas day at the in-laws, I excepted so as to please the misses, but was full of in trepidation, I had very little contact with my brother-in-law since that fateful encounter in the projection room, even on our wedding day when he was the elected one to give his sister away I steered clear of any contact, so here goes, grin and bear it. It was a strange day, my sister-in-law was at work until late afternoon so the day passed by with keeping two young nieces amused. By the late evening it was heavy snow, and quite deep by the time we made our way back home. The next day I trudged the two miles to work. Let's get that boiler stoked up, it was good to be back; thick snow outside and also on the screen with Kirk Douglas in 'The Heroes of Telemark'

KIRK DOUGLAS, RICHARD HARRIS
ARE ON A MISSION!

THE HEROES OF TELEMARK

I spent the day in the projection room on my own that day, it was great – sanctuary.

Over the next few months I spent many hours trying to persuade Geraldine that we should move away from this house (I just couldn't settle there) either to another town and another cinema or just another local location, she didn't like the idea and it was not going to be easy, but I knew we couldn't stay together under this roof.

A few months later I noticed an advert for a private bungalow for rent in the village of Shimpling eight miles out of Bury, I liked the sound of it and persuaded her to come with me and view the possibilities.

I asked the Manager to let me borrow his treasured mini to enable us to view the property. After collecting the keys from the owner, I fell for it at first glance, but could see the look of foreboding in her face, it was not going to be easy convincing her, but even she had come to realise the strain of living only a street away from her mother, was taking its toll on our lives, and she had this uncanny way of making her feel guilty if she didn't get a daily visit, that could last for hours. We had a long discussion, at times heated, within the confides of that empty property after which we agreed to give it a go. So the deal was done and a move date was made for two weeks' time. It was a quiet drive back to Bury, but inside I felt we had made the right decision, and couldn't wait to get moved and settled in.

Back at work I tackled some long awaited jobs with renewed relish, like clearing a store room of old projector parts so we could use it for other purposes, here I was lugging these old projectors to some other place at the rear of the cinema, God were they heavy, why do I get these mad ideas, ouch! That's another pulled muscle.

At home we were busy packing ready for our move, the mother-in-law was giving her a hard time, and I knew she was keeping that from me, but could feel the tension, soon be all over.

Sunday 8th April 1970 I had hired a transit van; David (my best man) and Marilyn who were now married, and I had reciprocated the roll for them, were on hand to help with the move. It was a long hard day but by the end of it after returning the van and David picking up his car we returned to Shimpling fait accompli.

The very next morning I suddenly realised the impulse of my actions, how the hell do I get to work, the only bus leaves at 8 a.m. and that was long gone, not to worry I'll walk to the main road then hitch a lift, I walked all the way to work, then had to repeat the process at the end of the day. On getting home I could see just how busy Gerry had been, things were looking very homely, she had met our neighbour, a widow Mrs Welham and struck up an instant friendship. We decided that I should catch the eight o'clock bus tomorrow, so I would only have one way to negotiate, trouble with that I didn't have to start work till eleven so it made it a long day. Some nights I managed to get a lift home, others I just hoofed it.

That weekend we noticed a car for sale an old Ford Consul only ten pounds, we scraped round and got the money, and I went to purchase the motor hoping it would be the answer to our prayers, as I drove away, I was feeling very pleased with myself, it didn't last long. Just a few miles down the road it came to an abrupt halt as the clutch had gone.

I had to get it towed to a garage for repairs, which meant more expense we didn't have capital for. I bussed back home feeling quite dejected, and set to mending Gerry's old bicycle, this would have to do for the time being and for the next week I cycled back and forth, it was better than walking, although after three days I knew I had a problem.

My groin was swollen and hurting and a visit to my doctor revealed a hernia (bet that was that muscle pull when we moved those old projector parts) the cycling was aggravating the hernia and I was put on a waiting list for repair surgery. By the end of the week we had enough to get the car out of the garage, on picking it up I was advised not to go on any long journeys as it was old and fragile, I was pretty naive but drove away very warily.

Over the next few weeks we settled down the old car was just about running I had taken to going by the back roads as the engine was smoking badly, I would have the bike in the boot, park just outside Bury and peddle in, then repeat it at night.

By now I was deputising on a Tuesday for the manager, and this particular day I had decided to go home at lunch time to break up the day as we had a later opening time, what a mistake that turned out to be. On the way home the front brakes suddenly started binding the drag made the engine smoke even more. I got home and spent the lunch hour freeing the brake shoes, then on my return trip, without warning the car lurched to one side and my front wheel went bouncing off in front of me, oh bugger! I had forgotten to tighten up the wheel nuts, it took them about three miles to work their way off, so there I was searching the ditch for my wheel then trying to get a bottle jack under the car that was sitting on the rim, it took ages and was one of the very rare occasions I have ever been late for a show.

During the week I was advised that a local garage had a Ford Thames Van for sale for only £40 a part exchange they wanted to clear, I had a look at it, and being the novice I was thought it was better than what I had. But forty pounds, that was two weeks' wages, and out of my reach. I was telling my ex landlady (Margaret) all about it, as she still worked as an usherette, and we often chatted over things, and to my astonishment she offered to lend me the forty pounds, in fact insisted, and I could pay her back at five pounds a week. The deal was done and the 1952 three speed Ford Thames van was mine, it turned out to be a reliable little workhorse, and a worthy investment.

Eddie and me taking Jason for a walk

It also meant we could go home to Ramsey and see them all, something we had not done for a long time and as Mum had been quite ill during and since the arrival of the latest family member, Adrian. I don’t think we ever knew just how close we had come to losing both of them.

Life had settled quite nicely and the country life suited us both. The Mother-in-law came over some weekends and all was happy. I was considering getting a few chickens, but only with the help of my dad. Home life was a refreshing change from being cooped up in a dark projection room all day, and the routine suited, just fine.

CHAPTER 16

Nothing lasts for long and the bubbles keep on bursting, Neal (David's brother) had just given notice, he never did really settle, the good news was that Eddy was now of age to become a 2nd projectionist, and not a trainee. Then it was Mr Millar on one of his rare visits to the cinema. I was called down to the office and told that the he would be selling the business on, we need not worry as all our jobs were safe, it was being sold as a going concern to another cinema operating company who wanted to expand their circuit into East Anglia. They were The Star Group of Companies based in Leeds and we would be seeing a flurry of their representatives over the next few weeks. Oh well we couldn't alter it so let's just see what develops.

In what seemed no time at all, Mr Millar bowed out and new work contracts exchanged hands with continued employment terms and conditions. The new faces that started to appear always seemed full of enthusiasm and promises of a bright and secure future, but why did they always talk about bingo! It was a dirty word within the cinema fraternity, as so many cinemas of the era were being lost to make way for this bingo craze; were we going to fall into this trap?

After a couple of uncertain months, of rumours running rife and Star Group people coming and going there was a staff meeting called and our future was mapped out for us. It seemed that on August 20th 1972 the cinema was to close for four months and be converted into two small studio-style cinemas and a bingo hall. The staff, with the exception of manager and projectionists were to be made redundant from this date, with the promise of re-employment when the new recruitments took place, it was a meeting with very mixed feelings and emotions, Geraldine had just got nicely settled into being a part-time usherette, which took the strain off the family budget, that was our bitter blow, the old van needed some new tyres, so we managed to scrape enough together beforehand and sort that out. The next few weeks just rocketed by, every day saw a new person with plans and tape measures all over the building, the residential area had now been vacated with the exception of the manager's bed-sit flat, and these were to be the first stage of the alterations, although the façade of the building was not to be altered in any way, it was a listed building. It seemed surreal to watch the old flats have the inner walls taken down; it was only a short few years ago that Geraldine had lived there

Now it was gone, the end of an era.

The final week of the Abbeygate, Walt Disney's 'The Aristocats' was to be our last film. During that week all the projection room furnishings and fittings that would not be needed were being dismantled ready for removal and storage, some of it would be re-used at a later date. Once the final show was out of the way and all the equipment stripped down and despatched, myself and Eddy became redundant as the projection room had been demolished, and the new one not yet constructed just the iron staircase up the side wall to a platform at the top. We just tried to keep out of the way, Eddy managed to get some extra work by helping the labourers, me I was glad of not being wanted for a week or two until new rooms had been built and needed fitting out, as Geraldine had become quite poorly and that was a worry, in the end it was decided to send for the doctor despite her protests, so the call was put out for a home visit. I would pop into work and check I was not needed then hot foot it back home before the Doc arrived, all going to plan then on the way back I ran over something in the road a Bang! from under the van, but all seemed OK. When I pulled up at home a strong smell of petrol and an instant puddle appeared under the stationary van, it had punctured the petrol tank, sod it, could have done without that. So there I was lying under the motor stinking of petrol and the doctor turns up, don't suppose he took much notice, but it made me very self-conscious as I showed him into the bedroom and Geraldine. I went for a quick scrub up whilst he did his examination, and the end result during the summing up was that she had become very anaemic and weak, with a lack of iron in the blood, and oh yes, "I think you are about two months pregnant." Along with the list of prescription items for pills and tonics and an appointment made to visit him at the surgery in a week's time, he made his leave, leaving two very shell-shocked people behind, pregnant the very last thing any of us had suspected.

Within a few days, after taking all the doses of potions and pills you could clearly see the transformation in her outward appearance, in fact one could say she started to blossom.

A week later there we were sitting in the waiting room of the doctor's surgery in Long Melford after her consultation; the pregnancy was fully confirmed and he was very pleased with her progress, more tonic and iron tablets, and the birth would be around mid-March. Arrangements would be made at the Bury Hospital and with the local mid wife.

Home life settled down after that and let me off the hook as baby talk and births is a 'girlie' thing. All I had to do was make the spare bedroom into a nursery. I wanted to paint a Disney mural on the wall, with lots of funny faces. Plenty of time to do it on my evenings off.

Back to work full time I had had three weeks of just popping in to see what progress had been made, but it was now time to start fitting out some of the completed areas and the newly constructed projection room was well underway. My old van was still chugging back and forth although I couldn't fill more than half-way or it would start leaking petrol, my repair was not that good, needed a new tank but it wasn't going to get one.

The general conversion was now taking shape the two studio cinemas were coming along I would check their progress several times during each day, as the concept of twin screens was still new to us, and the projection was to be beamed through mirrors (the periscope system) this would allow the projection room to be sited directly over the auditorium, beamed straight down for 20 feet then out to the screen. The new projection room was being constructed in what used to be the old roof void, it now had floors and walls, but still had the steel roof trusses running across, which you had to scramble over until the new steelwork was in place to allow a section to be cut out, this would then separate the room into two projection areas during the next month the work load started to intensify, it was only six weeks away from the opening date.

Young Eddy had become completely wrapped up in his newfound labouring capacity, he was being paid peace work, as well as the retainer wage we were getting; during the times we did get together for various jobs it became obvious the new technology and completely different method of projection was worrying him despite my reassurances. In a week's time the projection room would be ready for fitting out and the equipment that was taken away for storage would be returning along with the new long play film carriers a completely new piece of kit we had only seen in trade magazines, also new to us would be the projector light source these were going to be the new xenon lamps, instead of carbon arcs, our days would be long and fulfilling from then on assembling our own projection plant, then Stan the Westrex man would come along and complete all the intricate wiring, also connecting amplifiers and stage speakers.

November 5th 1971 a job I hadn't bargained for – I was going to have an early night in fact there was no one working that evening, when at 5 p.m. a delivery man put in an appearance and proceeded to unload 55 large battery cells onto the pavement together with racking and transformers, this was our emergency lighting unit that we had been waiting for, we had previously got ready a room to house this equipment, and here I was stuck with it, the staircase to the room had not yet been put in place, just a series of walkways of scaffold boards bouncing one up to the next level, oh well, sooner done and off the pavement the sooner I would be home, as promised.

Three hours later trudging up and down these walkways with fireworks going off outside overhead, I made my way home shattered, we would have to make up the rack and assemble the batteries into one large cell tomorrow that would then be the 110-volt emergency lighting system ready to connect in. That night once home and cleaning up, my jumper, shirt and vest just fell off me in shreds from where the battery acid had splashed on bouncing up those walkway boards. It don't get no better than this.

The next day after a good night's sleep I dropped the Mrs off at her mothers, and went to get a good start on assembling that battery rack, it had to be done as the engineer was coming that afternoon to complete all the connections, both myself and Eddy beavered away at this contraption only to realise that fully assembled it was four inches longer than the room it was to be housed in, where's the foreman, he had to get a chippy to cut a six inch recess into the wall cavity for us to complete the job, but luckily it was finished in the nick of time and by the end of day emergency lighting had been installed, and all 55 batteries were charging up nicely.

The next day the new steel support trusses would be arriving with a team of welders to fit them into place, then remove the obstructing sections that went directly across the projection room, as soon as that job was completed we could arrange delivery of our own equipment and come alive doing our own thing in fitting out the projection room.

Two days later a lorry turned up with all our projectors and kit; it's funny how suddenly there is an absence of people when you need extra hands to carry all this heavy equipment up to the very top of the building, but we managed and got it all under cover before the weather closed in on us.

Over the next week or so we both spent every spare minute building up a working projector, whereas before the projection method was to have two projectors which would run single reels and keep changing over to the different parts, we would now only have the one machine and this giant film carrier with spools that could carry 13,000 feet of film, a whole feature. It all seemed larger than life and towered above me.

Larger than life film carrier

Within four days we had the resemblance of two projection systems ready for Stan the Westrex man to come and do all the wiring and fitting of amplifiers for the sound, rectifiers for the xenon lamps and general testing, we also had two old feature films turn up for use as test films, it had been a long time since we had handled film, and it really felt good.

With only two more weeks to go before the opening day, panic seemed to have set in downstairs, the adjoining bingo hall was by far the largest area and nearly every day I seemed to be called upon to learn how certain pieces of equipment operated as it would be our job to maintain the combined unit after the opening, and all the workmen had gone.

I hadn't seen much of Mr Berry over the weeks but knew he was having a difficult time, the manager's position had vastly changed and he would have to oversee the bingo operation as well as the cinemas, something he just had no interest in, and just didn't want to do, he spent a whole afternoon pouring his heart out telling me how he felt and that a 'bingo' manager was coming down for a short stay to train him, oh dear.

The next day I was informed that the large periscope mirrors would be arriving, and once fitted we would be able to project an image onto the screens. The screens were my first disappointment; as they were both much smaller than I had been told, apparently the plans changed daily, and they were now solid screens of plasterboard skimmed and painted white, the entire frontage was white and this would be covered with lighting effects that hid the true size of the screen, our job to fit these in once the mirrors had been installed. I said to Eddy let's go home early have a good night then get an early start on it tomorrow. This we did

I trudged back to the car park to get my van only to find out that I'd left the headlights on after the foggy drive in that morning and the battery was as flat as could be, hang on this van had a starter handle, I had never tried it but this could be the big moment, how wrong I was, I wound that handle until my hands started to blister but with no battery it just wouldn't fire up, not a sole about either, I did try push starting it but couldn't get up any pace so as to jump in and put it in gear, by the time I got to that point, the bloody thing had stopped. Oh well, lock it up and bring a battery charger in tomorrow. Would have to taxi home tonight then catch the one and only bus into town at 8 o'clock in the morning I did say to Eddy "get an early start".

The very next day Geraldine decided that as it was Wednesday and market day she would ride in with me then spend the day with her mother until I picked her up, she was now five months gone and looking like a mum to be, it was another cold and foggy November morning as we got off that bus and walked back to the van where I took off the battery and carried it up to my projection room and put it on charge for the day. After a cuppa we parted company whilst we got ready for these mirrors to turn up, not quite sure what to expect, but no worries the company Engineer (Dennis Cheetham) and his assistant (Mark Woofindin) would be arriving with them and stay until the job was complete and we had a picture on each screen.

I had met both of these people before and had no cause to doubt their ability in installing this type of projection method. At ten o'clock a lorry with the Star Group emblem emblazoned across it pulled up out front, our first shock was the size of these things even taking account of the transit packing, four boxes two with studio One and two with Studio Two, four heavy duty backing plates, fixings and tension strainers, the largest mirror was 6' 8" X 4' 6" and weighed an absolute ton, it took five of us to get each one off the lorry and into their respective Studios. It was about that time I suddenly started to realise this conversion job was not all it seemed to be, we shall see.

About lunchtime the engineer and assistant put in an appearance and were quite pleased the humping of this equipment had been done. When all the niceties were over the truth started to dawn, in Studio One we all stood staring at this bloody great mirror, and this beautifully constructed periscope shaft that came straight through the ceiling from the projection room above, one problem the lower section that would house the largest mirror was only four foot square, obviously no one could believe their eyes, it was like a scene from a carry on film, everyone looking and pointing up then down for ages, then little huddles of workmen all whispering in unison, the works foreman was summoned then the on-site architect, we were just told they were going off for a meeting, back in an hour.

I went and got my now fully charged battery, thought I'd go and fit it back on the van in daylight, Eddy said he would help me carry it back, just going out the front doors and who's coming down the street lugging a bloody great sack of 'shallots' I nearly had a fit – five months pregnant and hauling these down the streets, with this triumphant beam on her face, before last month we never ate pickled onions. The van started first time so with her and the onions safely settled we proceeded to take her to the mother-in-law's for safe keeping, stopped for a quick cuppa then back to the mirror problem.

It turned out that two chippies would work overnight and dismantle the periscope structure and rebuild a much larger one, they had to wait for a tower scaffold to be erected, but should be done within 24 hours. OK let's have a look at Studio two we may get that one started, slide rules, tape measures and more huddles in corners, it seems the screen has been made too big for the mirror size and as you can't fit a larger mirror in the shaft provided, the only other option was to reduce the screen size, more unhappy chippies, they had worked hard on these areas and made a neat and sturdy job now they would have to hack it about, they were not happy, to say the least.

Our turn next, we had followed the plans to the letter when assembling the projectors, now they wanted the film carriers to be moved to the rear of the projector so as to move it forward, in that way the lens could be another five feet nearer the top mirror, thus reducing the image on the lower and much larger one. Stan was re-commissioned to spend the day with us the next day overseeing the operation as all the cables would have to be extended or moved, we were not amused, let's go home and have a fresh start tomorrow.

I went downstairs to have a chat with Mr Berry and let him know the latest; here was a man at the end of his tether, the strain clearly showing, he had just been informed that he would also be managing the bingo hall as well, after training. I also found out that a 'bingo' manager and his team would be arriving tomorrow from Northallerton a Mr Rosscamp, they would be recruiting new staff and starting a training schedule with immediate effect. I made my leave and went home feeling quite sorry for him, but I had enough problems of my own.

An evening off it seemed ages since we were at home together, it had been 'Bed and Breakfast' most days although we did have Sundays off, back to the spare bedroom come nursery, my mural was coming along nicely, Geraldine was busying herself with Christmas.

Hell, I hadn't given a thought to that, and it was only a month away, we would have to get home to Ramsey before the opening or else we would never make it, home life and work was a major juggling act at the moment, but the Mrs never complained, just took it in her stride, thank goodness.

Back at work the next morning, the overnight workers were just finishing off the hastily constructed periscope shaft, the original took a week to build, this looked a monstrosity hanging out of the ceiling, a real rush job. The morning was spent fitting the top cradle in place, then fastening the smaller mirror to it, now the BIG one that would sit in the box hanging below the ceiling, three of us sliding it up three ladders with a rope being pulled from the projection room some 30 feet up, talk about Health & Safety, it never entered into it, after much effort we eventually succeeded to get this contraption housed in the shaft, what a relief, I never felt safe up there, and that feeling was to last for years. Now to put a beam of light through and start the long laborious job of fixing strainers and angling the beam down to the screen, the company engineers did that whilst I concentrated on the light coverage first then the target film so as the get the lines straight, who was kidding who here, it looked like one of those funny mirror images you see at the fairground, ripples in the glass made a moving image shimmer, a still picture looked passable, but I was very disappointed with the overall result, despite being told by the so called technical engineer, "That's better than some I've seen." Now to install Studio Two; the screen size had been reduced dramatically overnight and again I had my reservations as the mirrors and fixings were being installed, the end result was better than I expected, although I was still bitterly disappointed after being led to believe we wouldn't know the difference. The unreal thing was looking through the projection porthole, all you could see was the screen, and not all of that, so strange when you were used to seeing your audience, and being able to gauge their reactions be it comedy, horror films, anything really, you could always get a feel of them enjoying the show you were projecting, that element had now been taken out of the job.

One week left before the opening day, downstairs was a hive of activity bingo callers being trained I could hear those numbers echoing around in my sleep, the cinemas were nearly ready now just a bit more carpeting and seating to complete, the cleaning team were frantically hovering and dusting each day as workmen scurried about their tasks leaving mess behind. That Rosscamp manager was strutting about like the big I am, rubbing everyone up the wrong way, Mr Berry had shut himself away from anything to do with bingo, and told me that once the place was up and running, he was off. I knew exactly how he felt, a cinema manager and a bingo manager are just two completely different type of persons, having previously had a run-in with Rosscamp over a cinema issue, I knew exactly what he meant.

The projection room was as ready as ever it could be, just waiting on the film prints to arrive; they duly did 'Paint Your Wagon' and 'Puppet On a Chain'.

Boxes of trailers and adverts, two days to get them all ready, no worries, spend today getting them made up onto these larger than life spools then tomorrow we would have a dummy run-through, but first of all just look at those mirrors, the bottom one was covered in dust, it would mean getting a two stage ladder out and climbing up to clean them, we would have this ritual every time they needed a clean, Studio Two wasn't so bad they were situated at the rear of the auditorium and could be reached off a step ladder, in fact one could crawl in the shaft and work above them.

Our first run-through went quiet well, although the projectors ran a little warm, well these were Kalee 20s, a heavy duty projector that was designed to run one off reels with a rest in between, now they were being asked to run continuous, and they didn't like it.

Opening day tomorrow, December 16th 1971 'Paint Your Wagon' and

'Puppet On a Chain' a full day's projection once again.

"Stake your claim to the Musical goldmine of '69'"
Lee Marvin, Clint Eastwood & Jean Seberg

PAINT YOUR WAGON

From the author of "Guns Of Navarone", "Ice Station Zebra" & "Where Eagles Dare"
Alistair MacLean's

PUPPET ON A CHAIN

CHAPTER 17

The opening started off with complete panic, downstairs that was, Eddy and me did a tour round the building checking the heating, ventilation and that all the lights were working, and just watched all the bingo staff running about in ever decreasing circles, we took our leave and departed to the sanity of the projection room, anyway there was for the next two days an electrician and all round workman on site, just in case the building started to fall apart or anything went bang! The day went well, no projection problems, downstairs in screen one an elderly lady fell over, a 'step trip' and had to be taken off by ambulance. Apparently the bingo blower (hoover motor attached to a long clear plastic tube) how technical, well it stopped running half way through a game, and the next ball with the numbers on didn't come up the tube. I think about fifty people all shouted in unison that they would have had the next number as a winner. After a few hectic days things started to settle down into a routine, Christmas was not far away, luckily Geraldine had been busy getting it all together, I hadn't even given it a thought. Mr Berry told me that Christmas Eve was to be his last day; he was leaving, rather than become associated with bingo. Things were certainly changing.

Christmas came and went, just the one day off, Geraldine did the visiting rounds with her family members, I would pick her up and off home we would go, at the end of the show. During the first week of January we were informed that Friday nights would be Late Shows starting at eleven o'clock, the Licence had been duly granted so off we jolly well go, going to be a long day, the first film would be Jane Fonda and Donald Sutherland in 'Klute', it was nothing special, but the novelty factor of a cinema being open into the small wee hours attracted a large audience, I remember saying to Eddy, "They won't be dropping these in the near future." He was courting quite strongly now and was becoming increasingly disillusioned with the job, especially when I had a day off, and he couldn't get a break. After a few weeks he dropped the bombshell, he was leaving; he wanted something with more regular hours, evening and weekends off.

It was about this time I was looking for another motor, with a new baby on the way we really needed something better than the van, someone I knew whose father owned a garage and used car saleroom in Woolpit would keep his eye open for me, only a few days later he rang to tell me that they had taken in a part exchange car that was in good clean condition, a Vauxhall Victor Estate it was massive, column gear change, bench seats but ran like a dream, it was ours by the end of the day.

My trusty old motor, a real workhorse

They didn't want the van, no surprise there, so it had to be relegated onto a piece of waste ground next to the bungalow.

During the latter part of January we noticed the picture area on screen would change shape during the day and by the last show would be creeping up the screen, something that was to dog me for years to come. The structure of the periscope shaft was all fire treated timber and was still quite wet when built, it now seemed it was drying out and changing shape which in turn put pressure on the mirror cradles and twisted the glass, very slightly but enough to effect the image projecting through it, certain weather conditions made it worse, it meant we would come in a morning climb up to the large bottom mirror, shoot a white light onto the screen then by manipulating the mirror which laid on this swivel cradle try to get a complete picture area on the screen, one slight movement of the glass and the screen image would move by about six inches, by packing pieces of card under the mirror to compensate the structure movement, after a painstaking time and effort we would have a plausible coverage of the screen below, clean the mirror then carefully get out of the shaft and down the ladder without any sudden movement. Unfortunately this periscope was situated in the middle of the auditorium, protruding out of the ceiling, trouble was it acted like a great big funnel and sucked up all the smoke, dust and heat. By mid-evening the picture was noticeably on the move, back to square one.

The end of the week was fast approaching and Eddy would be off, this was going to be tough we had no one lined up to take over from him the bingo manager Rosscamp was no help what so ever, kept promising to place adverts, but nothing ever appeared. Our baby was due in about six weeks' time and I wanted an assistant projectionist by then for obvious reasons. A couple of weeks passed and I was completely on my own long hard days plus Friday night Late Shows, and nursing these blessed mirrors on a daily basis I was getting to the end of my tether with it all, my Diamond Girl never once complained, I think that made me feel even more guilty.

Friday night halfway thru the Late show 'Shaft' with Richard Rowntree, what's that burning smell! Turned out after a rush investigation the projector drive belts were so hot from friction they were actually smoking, now what? About the same time it was noticed that the sound was warbling, that means the projector is running slow. Kalee 20's a heavy duty projector, all the gears and shutter shafts are sealed in an oil bath, as I said before would run for years on the old two projector system, but now they never got a rest, and with the intense heat of these xenon lamps, this one was in the early stages of seizing up on me, and the motor was working extra hard to keep it all turning over, hence the friction and burning belts, with cooling fans trained onto the projector, it limped through the film, despite becoming very flickery towards the end. Luckily we had some spare projector heads in stock (someone must have foreseen this) so despite a late finish, it would be an early start tomorrow to replace the head before we could start a show.

A couple of days later quite out of the blue the ex-projectionist from the Odeon paid me a visit as he had never seen the large reel film carriers, it was during this visit that he let slip he wouldn't mind doing some part time work back in projection, I don't think I quite bit his hand off, but a deal was struck before he left the building, two evening a week, after an initial shift to familiarise him with the equipment and switch gear, then an evening off to look forward to.

This was better, two evenings a week off I could get my mural finished, time was getting short the due birth date was only a week away, never mind I had some help now and he said he would do some extra hours at the time.

CHAPTER 18

March 23rd 1972 a bright sunny morning, I was just contemplating the day ahead from my horizontal position in bed, when in she waddled and said I think you need to ring the hospital, today could be the day! I was out of that bed and down to the village phone box in a trice, Panic, what me! Only to be told in the most reassuring voice – bring her down at your leisure, no rush. Believe me she was in that car and down the road before she knew what was happening to her.

It was now 10 o'clock and she was all checked in and settled, in those days it was not encouraged that you should stay, and to be present at the birth was unheard of, so I had to take my leave although early I made my way to work, at least it was my evening off, I could get home to see our dog Jason, Mrs Welham was going to see to him during the day so as I could be at the hospital for as long as need be.

The day dragged on, two long films 'Ben Hur', a re-issue as they called them, and 'Soldier Blue'.

Charlton Heston
Is

BEN HUR

Once these got running there was not a lot to do but machine watch for couple of hours. During the afternoon I made my pre-arranged call to the maternity ward, nothing doing yet, just be patient, oh well better get upstairs, I know watch a bit of Ben Hur that should take your mind off things, it was during this that the internal house phone started ringing off the wall, here goes, this is it, but no it was the assistant manager informing me that my projectionist had just rung in sick, thanks a bunch mate, I stomped around cursing the job, the bingo-minded management, the company, everything and everybody, but it didn't change anything I was still lumbered, I again rang in for an update report, only to told, very little change, but all is well, left a message that I would be there as soon as the show closed. It was a long night, two long films as well. At last ten thirty did tick round and I raced straight to the hospital where I was taken into a side ward, and there she lay looking quite relaxed despite the pains that kept on coming in waves, after about an hour I was told they would be taking her to a delivery room and I would have to leave. There was a waiting room that I could go to until it was all over. I opted to go for a drive, and went to inform the in-laws what the state of play was.

I arrived back at 11.50 p.m. to be told I was the father to a healthy baby boy, and I could see him and his mother in due course. What a day!!

I crawled home at three in the morning to be met by a very grateful dog, and after a while just crashed out.

In what seemed no time at all it was 'up and at em'
And the realisation suddenly set in that life would never be the same again, a visit next door to give our neighbour Mrs Welham the latest update, she was the only one I had to inform, as I knew that in a few hours the news would be all over the village, give Jason a good walk over the fields, put some finishing touches on my wall mural, then off to work, Friday, late show day, gonna be a long one.

My boy's bedroom

A labour of love

Once at work I managed to use the office phone to ring for an update, all was well, my relief should be on duty this eve, so I should be able to make a visit. The day went well the part time projectionist rang in to say he was feeling better and would be in this evening, but could only work until 10.30 p.m. and not the Late Show, blast! Well at least I could get a visit in, you had one hour and that was it, goodness knows when I would get in again, no more relief until Tuesday evening, and they might be home by then. The next two days seemed like a prison sentence, apart from one call each day to check on their progress I was stuck. I know she wasn't short of visitors over the weekend but it didn't make me feel any better. On the Monday I had formulated a plan, with the help of the assistant manager, that was because we had two very long films running, I would set the matinee running and once the main features were on screen shoot off to pay a surprise visit, and be back before the reels ran out, if anything should go wrong he would have to throw the mains switch to that system, and wait for me to return. I must say I was a bit worried about leaving both shows unattended but the overwhelming desire to see my family won the argument, and I must say all went well, and I felt more content than the previous days.

Tuesday the big event they were coming home, and I had the evening off, and life was just fine, work had settled into a steady routine, just a few mishaps and breakdowns to liven us up, just needed a full time projectionist to complete the set-up.

Our valued neighbour Mrs Welham

Night time feed with Stuart

Proud mum, bless 'em both

A few weeks passed by and I was called down to the manager's office and asked how I would feel if Stan Boxshall came in as my second projectionist, now this was Stan the Westrex engineer who I had worked closely with since coming to Bury, and learnt a great deal on the technical aspects of the job from him, he was now retired from Westrex and looking for a full time job, well I had never seen him do any projection work, only repairs and maintenance; he could be just what we need, at least I could get some complete days off and become 'a family man' so why not give him a trial run, "That's good," he said. "He starts next Monday."

After only a couple of days Stan was in his element two projectors and all the ancillary equipment to play with, he spent the entire days just tinkering with them, the only problem was when Stan looked at a running projector in his mind's eye he could only see gears and sprockets turning, he just couldn't get the hang of concentrating on the output picture along with the presentation techniques, never mind I could live with that, he could only improve and I was to have two days off next week, it would be like a mini holiday, and I needed a break.

The next Tuesday soon came round and over the weekend we had a letter from my mum & dad, they would like to visit on Tuesday as well, just for a couple of hours they had someone to drive them over I think they really just wanted to see the new addition to the family, and what a day off it was. I was telling dad of my plans to build a chicken house and have a few chickens, he said he would come over for a few days when it was built and help me choose some from the cattle market.

Work had settled down nicely but the part-timer had given notice, couldn't keep up the pace of two jobs, so that left Stan and Me and things seemed to be running along quite well. Stan had rigged up a pulley system at the very top of our iron staircase so we could raise and lower the full cases of film, save carrying them all the way up and down. It all seemed to be working OK although I thought one strained more muscles heaving a heavy case up in the air, I'm sure it was easier just carrying them, but hadn't the heart to say anything, until that one fateful night when well after the show we had packed all the reels into the metal transit case, last job get it downstairs ready for collection then we could lock up and go home, the film was Lee Marvin in 'Prime Cut'.

LEE MARVIN and GENE HACKMAN
TOGETHER THEY'RE MURDER IN

PRIME CUT

We took the full case outside to the top platform of the staircase hooked on the rope and swung it off the ledge so as to lower it down, when suddenly the handle gave way on the case and it went crashing down to earth, I rushed down to check the damage and shouted up to Stan, "I think we have got away with it," but on closer inspection all five reels within the case had flattened out on impact, the plastic bobbins had crushed along with the bottom of the tins when you managed to get a tin out of the case it looked like a large letter D, we had to take them back upstairs and whilst Stan was tapping the tins out to resemble a circular shape I was winding the film onto a new bobbin, not an easy task with the shape they were in, it was well gone midnight when we finally got away, and the rope and pulley was never used again.

It was good getting regular days off, life at home was bliss and I could busy myself in the garden and building a chicken house, on my next day off I would travel to Ramsey and bring Mum, Dad & Adrian back for a few days, and dad and me could go to the Wednesday cattle market and get some chickens so as to stock up my newly built chicken house, good job he was with me, all those cages of chickens, chicks, geese everything you could imagine, we chose the ones that interested us, well Dad did really, I just followed on, then it was time to wait for the auction, another new experience and a world away from being in a projection room, but it was a laugh. Dad came up trumps and bidded for our chosen two pens of chickens four Rhode Island reds and six bantams, plus a cockerel thrown in for good measure I immediately named him 'Foghorn Leghorn' (film influence again) much to my father's bemusement. Once paid for and boxed up we triumphantly trundled our way home to show them off. Over the next few days I was checking them every few hours; where's the eggs? Only to be told that they are out of season, not in lay that's why we got such a good price deal, be patient and in a few weeks they would come on to lay again, give them plenty of grit and bran in the meantime. Good old Dad, I wouldn't have had a clue, the only chickens I had seen lately were on screen, usually in a western, and they were always just laying eggs. A few weeks later a state of excitement existed as our first eggs starting coming off the production line, so to speak.

Easter over, and the summer to look forward to with some long country walks with my son and the dog, who could have wanted for anything more.

Work had settled into a routine, bingo was still the driving factor, cinema business being very mediocre made any requests for improvements fall on very deaf ears. I seemed to spend my working days either at loggerheads with managers or with the help of Stan mending broken down pieces of equipment. At least the experimental Friday Late shows had now run their course and been discontinued. So for once in my life I could put my energies into home life, and play 'Happy Families' that would take us up to the christening in September.

CHAPTER 19

As another year draws to a close Christmas took on a whole new meaning this was to be our first with a nine month old, who by now had taken on a character all of his own, I don't know which of us was the more excited, twinkling lights and pretty decorations. As I had previously said work life had become dull to say the least, cinema business all over had gone into meltdown, much to the bingo management's delight, so it was decided to have a family end of the year then see what the new year would bring. Myself and Stan would split the Boxing Day and New Year's Day shift between us, so two days off for Christmas never been known before, the films on offer were non inspiring Gene Wilder in 'Willy Wonka & the Chocolate Factory' and the alternative screen a double Elvis re-issue 'Girls Girls Girls' plus 'Paradise Hawaiian style'.

Shortly into the new year Stan dropped a bombshell and said he would be leaving at the end of the month, he had given it a good shot, but now needed more time at home. Here we go again just when I had got used to having regular time off, never mind perhaps a new projectionist would be forthcoming, who was I kidding cinema work was not considered the thing to do, and the adverts went without trace even the further afield ones in the trade press. By early summer I had become quite despondent having worked the past three months without a break, however I had arranged two weeks' holiday, and there would be a temporary relief projectionist drafted in, I really needed to get away and this was it, we had booked a chalet on the east coast not too far away, but far enough, even invited the mother-in-law as a thank you for all the baby sitting. My last working day before my holiday, waiting in anticipation for my relief to arrive, as the clocked ticked into the evening hours that feeling of doom started to take over, then about nine o'clock the internal phone rang to inform me that my relief had arrived and was with the bingo manager; turned out they were both from his home town. As the show came to a close I had still not met up with my relief, and after speaking to him on the house phone to ask if he would like a guided tour around all the switch gear and quirkiness of our projection system before I depart, but no, he had the spare keys from the office and was off to the pub with the Rosscamp crew see you in two weeks, with that I was in my car and away.

We would have the first few days catching up on some home jobs, a couple of days out, then away first thing Saturday morning, the weather had been improving daily and by now was just right for the seaside, in an elated state we all set out and had a most enjoyable week which went by much too quickly and it was time to go home, back to work tomorrow.

After two weeks away you always wonder what is waiting for you upon the return, I was not going to be disappointed, upon entering the projection room it looked as if a bomb had gone off, bits of broken film, fast food cartons and paper cups everywhere just a complete unkempt mess, a look at the projection mirrors showed they had not been touched

For two weeks, the picture quality must have been deteriorating daily, around mid-morning I was downstairs bemoaning the state of affairs to the assistant manager, who informed me, the relief projectionist went home last night so you won't see him at all, and during the day all I kept hearing was the horror stories of the two weeks gone by, films breaking down, shows not starting at the proper times, and to top it all young Eddy popped in to see me, turned out that on my first day away he and his girlfriend were in the audience to watch the Sunday matinee, after half an hour sitting there waiting for the show to start one of the usherettes asked if he would go up to the projection room and help the relief get the projector started, as the film kept breaking each time he tried. By the end of the day I had heard so many horror stories, I needed another holiday.

A few weeks passed by, still no second projectionist and I was beginning to get restless and despondent, my equipment kept letting us down and took up a lot of time just maintaining it and keeping it in running order, the projection mirrors had an overnight replacement done, I was still very disappointed with the result, and made my feelings known, only to be told I was too much of a perfectionist, and needed to be less critical, in other words nothing else was going to be done. We decided to alter our adverts and go for a non-experienced person, so as to train up from scratch, at least after a few weeks I could have him running a show at a basic level, and I could have a few hours off.

In the meantime this feeling of restlessness kept eating away at me, I knew the family did not want to move away, but I had had enough and wrote off in answer to a trade advert for a projectionist's position at Leamington Spa; the baby was being looked after by friends for the day, so just me and the misses, but as the journey progressed and the distance from Bury became ever further I could see and feel the change coming over her, how could I do it knowing what effect it was having, but I was committed now, no harm in having a look. Upon arrival and a meet with the owners it turned out the placement was already taken, but they could offer me a similar position some 25 miles further up country at Warwick, this was another of their cinemas that needed a projectionist and the position would be mine if I accepted it, we had come this far so might as well go and give it a once over. It was not for me; quite run down and unkempt is my best description, so after a very short look round we made our leave, and headed for home. Funny thing, a good long drive gives you time to mull many things over in the mind and I decided to get back and make the most of what I had and see how things went from there, all in all a good day's experience in work management.

Back to the reality of work, which I now saw in a different light, interviews galore to deal with, the advert for A non-experienced projectionist, as training would be given 'on the job', had opened the floodgate

After seeing the first batch, it was all becoming a much for much likeness so I decided on one person who came over as more interested than the rest, 'Bill', so the deed was done and his training would start in earnest, the very next day.

Working life certainly seemed a lot brighter, maybe it was having company and the challenge of training, a novice at an unusual pace, but Bill never wavered and turned out to be the right choice. Some time off now, half days to start with, then perhaps a full one in a week or so, it certainly made home life much better and to top that I was suddenly told that the Rosscamps would be leaving at the end of the month, and a new bingo manager would be taking over, well it couldn't be any worse, and the thought of another manager certainly made the day seem much brighter.

CHAPTER 20

In what seemed like no time at all, I was called to the office and introduced to this very tall, slim, mid-twenties chap. Ron McDaid a single fellow who had just left the Army and this was to be his first taste of civilian working life, it was soon obvious that he would need friends and guidance as he had no previous knowledge of our business, but was full of enthusiasm and had an avid interest in films; of course he felt rather torn between bingo and cinema as he had inherited the Rosscamp team and their working patterns and felt a little overawed with them all. He would often come up to the projection room for a chat and a cuppa, in fact we forged a good working relationship, and I started to learn quite a few management aspects to the job, and even put into practice a few ideas of my own, unfortunately this was not well received with the cinema staff downstairs for over the past years they had been allowed to do their own thing so long as the bingo operation was not involved, now all of a sudden their work practices were being challenged, and they didn't like it, the new manager was, in their eyes, a jumped up twit.

Things had certainly turned a full circle in such a short span of time, projectionist Bill had come on leaps and bounds, and was by now a reliable partner, which in turn allowed me to perform some duties downstairs to help Ron out.

The only blot on the landscape was that my home life was struggling mostly due to us having to survive on my lowly income, in those days there were no benefits for a first born, and as we lived out of town part time work for the wife was out of the question, and this was a constant worry to me, after several weeks searching I found an advert for a part time delivery driver 5 a.m. – 8 a.m. six days a fortnight, a bulk newspaper delivery round; I could handle this, it would not interfere with my cinema works, after a quick interview the job was mine. There was two of us doing a week on week off routine. The round consisted of a sixty-mile round trip starting off at WH Smiths warehouse in Bury followed by a dash off to meet the five thirty train at Stowmarket station where all the dailies had been bundled up ready for distribution. Eight drops in total all numbered and ready to add to the ones previously picked up from Smiths. After getting these off the train onto a trolley – juggling for position, there was about ten others all doing the same exercise, all wanting to be first away – once loaded it was off to Brandon my first of four stops in that area, then onto Weeting, Feltwell, Methwold, and finally Northwold, back to Bury, park up the van and decide home or work. If we had jobs on I would go in and get an early start, but on other days back home by nine o'clock sometimes to catch a couple of hours' sleep.

As the extra income started coming in, it was all worth the extra effort and made life much more comfortable, luckily this job started in April so it was always those nice light mornings and I use to love driving through the forest areas seeing the early morning roe deer, rabbits, badgers, etc., scurrying away from the roadside. As the autumn then winter months set in it became a different world November became a fog bound month, it seemed nearly every day it was thick fog, the train was always late and it seemed to be getting harder to wake up in the mornings. I would get in from the cinema at about eleven at night and have to be up and out by four thirty, it was getting harder, but we needed the money, then this one fateful morning as I was driving between Stowmarket and Brandon I must have momentarily dozed off on this straight stretch of road. It was a typical country road with water gullies cut out to allow drainage to the ditches, well the van ran into one of these shot into the air then into another gully, in the few seconds it took to get the van under control my life flashed before me, and I continued the journey very gingerly and wide awake, until I opened the van door at my first drop. My eight neatly numbered piles were just one large bundle, it took ages to sort it all out, a couple of months later on one of those artic frosty mornings everything was going to plan when between Weeting and Feltwell when the van just ground to a halt. After several attempts to locate the problem and try to get some life into the van I decided, as I was about half a mile from my next stop, that I would take a bundle of papers and walk in. There I could telephone for assistance; it was during that walk you could actually hear the frost forming in the hedge rows. It turned out the diesel had frozen in the pipelines.

Within eighteen months the cracks were beginning to show. Poor old Ron was under so much pressure to put more effort into the bingo operation, and spend less time with the cinema routine – the regional manager's suggestion. Although we had less time talking through each other's problems it was very noticeable that he was not so happy with his lot than when he first took up the position. He had also become very close to one of the staff in the bingo hall, Diane, and I would often have a social drink with them after the day's work. It was during one of these occasions they informed me that they were getting married and moving away all in about two months' time, oh dear just when things were going well.

The paper round was also coming to an end, the private transport firm was about to fold, and with it the job, I'm not sure if I was sorry or relieved as it had become a chore, but we still needed that money. Then that doors and windows syndrome again I was told about a part time vacancy at the bury mini bus company well why not the hours were better seven till ten five days a week, after an introductory visit the job was mine, start Monday, and of course you will have to have a medical and a PSV licence so a test will be arranged.

Monday soon came around and for the first trip I would have someone with me, the job was two trips each morning the seven thirty pickups were to ferry factory workers into town from some very obscure outlying places, deposit them at work then be at the next pick up point by eight fifteen, this time the school run, again from obscure places that full size buses couldn't get to. Despite the job being more suitable I was never that taken with it, I did get my PSV licence, and carried out a few trips on my days off.

Back at the cinema Ron & Dianne's wedding was looming near, then they would be off, a temporary manager was being put in place, here we go again.

I was not far wrong, two hours later than expected this motorcycle came chugging into the back yard and what can only be described as an unshaven ragged looking person came through the doors and blurted out, "I'm the new manager, where's the office?" Well the few staff that were around just stood open mouthed they just couldn't believe what had just happened was this really the new manager.

I made a sharp exit back to the projection room and waited for the proverbial to hit the fan.

Shortly after this the house phones started ringing, it was Claudine & Albert who were about the last two surviving members of the Rosscamp team.

They told me that they had applied to take over from Ron McDaid, but they were only interested in bingo, and would I help them run the cinema's? I responded by saying let's wait and see and we can discuss it when the time comes, a very shrewd move as it turned out.

The weeks passed by slowly, Claudine with Albert's assistance held the bingo operation together, whilst I attended to many of the administration jobs connected to the cinemas. As for this so called manager he would wander in at all odd times in full motorcycle regalia, shut himself in the office until he thought he had done enough, then just wander back out.

What a strange situation, it stood out a mile, it couldn't last for long, but it was nearly four months before he just left one night and never returned. These were funny old times and decisions made no sense at all as a succession of relief managers kept coming and going, Thereafter Claudine and Albert did a husband and wife team and took the reins, these being the only surviving members of the Rosscamp era.

Then without warning we were all informed that the company had just lost its gaming licence and EMI would be taking over the bingo operation within the next few weeks, but this would not include the cinemas, from all I could ascertain from the then regional manager on his visit is that the cinemas were to be closed down and boarded up for the time being. Despite that the Star company was still going to operate some of its cinema only stock, Bury was not included as it was a shared building and EMI were not interested in the cinemas, and it was so far from their Leeds base it held no interest.

I immediately made contact with the Star Group of Companies head office in Leeds, and offered my services to manage the cinemas, only to be told, "We don't accept projectionists in management positions." After the initial despondent feeling had passed by I started to bombard them with ideas, and a plan of action to implement. Within two weeks I was called to a meeting and again put forward a passionate plea for the continuance of the cinema business, and after a lengthy discussion it was agreed our two screens would be brought into the fold and we would have a review in six months, and if the business was still loss-making, it would then be curtains.

I wanted to give this my best shot and that meant no time for two jobs, the buses had to go; I was not that sorry to give notice.

CHAPTER 21

So in February 1975 I stepped into the manager's roll, full of trepidation and bright ideas, from the off I knew it was going to be difficult, the bingo staff were still using the cinema as a convenience and a shortcut through the premises, the staff I was to inherit were not very taken with the idea of me coming down to take over full time, they had over the years got a nice little regime set up all to their own advantage, and not always in the best interest of the cinema, things had to change if we wanted a future, and I knew then I had a fight on my hands. Bill was the only projectionist and I would have to relieve him for some time off until another one could be found, to do this I would need the other staff to be on side, and not see me as a threat, my very first staff meeting was called in two days' time when I listened intently to their views and fears for the future. After laying myself bare before them and explaining just what had taken place with the company to keep the cinemas open, they confessed they had no idea this had happened and by the end of the meeting all had agreed to work alongside me and accept that some changes would have to be made. The first few days were spent segregating the building from the bingo hall pass doors and dual routes were sealed up, much to the annoyance of the bingo staff. I think I was viewed as a jumped up prat, I could handle that, as my own staff now knew I meant what I said at our meeting.

Our first full film week was about to start we had a local themed film

Akenfield

PETER HALL'S FILM BASED ON RONALD BLYTHE'S BOOK

and from day one knew we had something special here; full houses day after day it just all seemed to fit into place and silenced the doubting mouthpieces once and for all, the weeks just seemed to be flying by, so much to learn and I spent many hours after the show pondering over the company work manual, the need to get it right was so strong failure was not an option I had managed to get myself a typewriter and one of those new electronic calculators that would take the strain off the ready reckoner.

Finding a projectionist to partner Bill was paramount he was a single lad and needed his time off, and I couldn't keep up the pace of relieving him and being a manager for much longer, then out of the blue a person came asking if we had any vacancies in projection, he used to work at the local Odeon and was looking for work, after a tour of the set up and some time to get to know Bill it was decided to give him a try on equal terms, as after a couple of shifts to familiarise himself with the equipment they would work opposite each other and I would continue to oversee the technical aspects with them.

Shortly after I met up with Frank the Chief projectionist of the Odeon, whom I had known since coming to Bury and had a good colleague based friendship with. When I told him of our latest addition he shrunk back in horror and said, "He was most unreliable when I had him," but for the moment he was just what we needed and relieved me of being burdened with the chore, I could now concentrate on business matters.

We were now into our third month, and I was to meet the Operations Manager of the company Bernard Morris, we hit off an instant friendship and his help and guidance over the next few years were invaluable, from an operational view I needn't have worried as once I started looking back into the cinema finances I discovered that many of the bingo overheads had been offset against the cinema income, no wonder we could never get anything repaired or renewed, our budget was always in the red, whilst the bingo flourished, so we could hold our own, even during the leaner months. Following on from that meeting it was decided to get the most senior cashier to stand in for me on two evenings a week, he was a little shocked to say the least that I hadn't had any time away since taking the management position.

Life at home had become a bed & breakfast role, but there had never been anything said although I knew they must have been longing to have some time with me at home or even an away day, we hadn't been home to Ramsey for ages, perhaps one evening next week, that would surprise them, must see about having a telephone fitted as well, as the weeks passed by it became obvious Frank was correct the projectionist we had taken on was as unreliable as ever, and it often seemed to correspond with my early evening off, that he or someone for him would phone him in sick, he had to go, the fragile structure was breaking down, after the demise of him we had a succession of oddball characters all purporting to be projectionists, it became difficult at times, problems in the projection room permeate throughout the building, and living a half hour drive away didn't help when you had to rush back and sort a problem, an alarm going off in the middle of the night was a particular problem.

In July I was asked by the company if I would go over to Colchester and re-open the Cameo Cinema this had been closed for a week due to a mass staff dismissal programme taking place, and they wanted someone to guide the remaining staff into becoming self-sufficient, I would go into my own site first thing and do the necessary needed to get it operational for the day then my own staff would oversee it until my return, then I would drive to Colchester meet the staff and get that up and running, well what a shock.

I had no idea just how run down this cinema was, it could only be labelled as a 'sex' cinema because that is what it had become. A strange building to say the least, it appeared to be built into the side of a hill and the auditorium was below street level, I had arrived in good time well before any staff and let myself into the foyer, it was as described, a small dingy space with a box office and kiosk to the left and a few steps across a door marked manager, as I turned the key I heard this scurrying from beyond and opening the door into complete blackness I stepped in only to go sprawling down onto the floor, I wasn't expecting a step down. After getting over the shock and finding a light switch I realised there were several steps down and the top of the desk was level with the bottom of the door and the desk top was covered in mice droppings (what had I come to) after looking over the building to familiarise myself with the layout, the auditorium could only be described as a long dark tunnel, the exit stairs went upwards until reaching street level.,

I never did find the projection room. It was now the arranged time to meet the staff three of, who actually turned out to be very nice people, it seemed the 'bad apples' had been ousted. I spent the afternoon listening to their horror stories, and noticing the regular possession of males that kept coming in asking for people who no longer worked there, yes it had been a glorified knocking shop and the film posters and titles all over the frontage wasn't going to make it easy to get the message over that the business had ceased. To make matters worse as I sat in the box office you looked out of the front windows and directly opposite was the plush ABC Cinema frontage. Around mid-afternoon the show was well underway with a handful of the 'dirty mac brigade'.

I asked how you got to the projection room, we had a picture on screen so someone had to be manning it and I wanted to know who. The directions were: out the front, walk up the hill, turn right and knock on the second door, it has Cameo written on it. Off I went and yes there was the door, knock knock, wait, knock again then the drawing of a bolt and this little fellow who seemed to have come out of the woodwork says "What you want?" After explaining Who I was and that I would like a look round and ask a few questions in I went into another pitch dark corridor, why so dark I asked, "No one ever comes in here." Towards the end of this passage I could hear that familiar sound of a projector ticking over, and here they were two Kalee 12s with Vulcan arcs a real step back in time.

Good old Bert who had been there years and now just locked himself away from all the goings on in his projection empire. The first thing I noticed was that there was quite a distinct downward angle from the projector, it seemed strange when you knew you had just walked in off the street, so Bert went into this talk of the history of the building and how indeed it was built into a hill side with the majority of the interior being underground. He turned out to be a very knowledgeable person, who had just lost his way, once told of the recent happenings within the cinema you could feel his interest returning, and he agreed to attend a staff meeting tomorrow. After returning to the foyer and explaining a plan of action to the two ladies I went to Woolworths and purchased several mouse traps and promised to set them up before I went, and I would be in first tomorrow so they wouldn't have to deal with them. So, with the plan in place they would lock up tonight. I took my leave and proceeded back to base. In the days that followed there was a coming together of the staff, even Bert elected to come out of his hidey hole and assist the girls with routine jobs. I don't think he had ever been asked before and now suddenly he felt part of a new team, even if only to empty the mousetraps each morning. This practice went on for about ten days and by that time I was needed less and less, and would often just direct them from my base cinema some forty miles away. Soon after a new manager was installed I was relieved of the duty, but alas some six months later it closed its doors and another cinema bit the dust.

It was about this time we had our first real tester with a Canadian film 'When the North Wind Blows' from Sun file Distributors.

“Together they faced the challenge of the Wilderness”

Henry Brandon, Herbert Nelson and featuring Dan Haggerty

WHEN THE NORTH WIND BLOWS

They did what was known as a ‘four wall deal’ whereby they paid up front a guaranteed sum of money to have their film shown for fourteen days and in return they would claim the remaining box office receipts. At that time this pot of gold seemed like a king’s ransom, and deals were done. Then something happened that we had never seen before, TV advertising. It seemed every time you switched on the television there was a trailer for this film. A media that had always been blamed on the cinema demise, was now being used in its favour, a new era was about to dawn.

Upon arriving at the cinema a queue was already lining the street, and this went on all day and every day for the entire fourteen days the queue became a permanent fixture, and it just moved up after each performance and waited for the next, much to the bemusement of our neighbours, especially the polish hairdresser next door, GEORGE, he would get most upset with all these people whiling away the time staring in his windows and pulling faces at the ladies having their hair set.

As the winter months had well set in I even coerced the wife to help out in the box office on the occasions that I had a shortage of staff and had to do projection work as well, that move turned out to be a great asset, not only was it someone to discuss problems with, but she had experience from the old Abbeygate days, the Mother-in-law was in her element looking after our son Stuart, she now had a purpose in life, and we saw a little more of each other, even if in a work context so I could start concentrating on the more pressing problems.

February 1976 we awoke to about a foot of snow, and it was still falling, luckily the Mother-in-law was spending the weekend with us as we both had to work this day, getting there was the first hurdle the village was about three miles off the main road and completely snowed in so we slipped and slid our way up the narrow village road trying to keep in the tractor ruts that had gone on before, noticing how the snow on the fields was being whipped into drifts by the wind, but after about an hour’s travel we eventually made it to work, not that there was any business about that day, no one seemed to want to venture out, anyway who wanted to see 'Caligula', the snow fell steadily on and off most of the day. At ten o'clock it was time to make our way home, once out of the town limits and into the countryside the journey got more and more difficult the drifted snow and been cut through with snow ploughs and we kept moving albeit very slowly until it came time turn off the main road, a few hundred yards down this road the snow we had witnessed earlier in the day drifting nicely across the open fields had now deposited itself onto the road, the first drift we hit head on and managed to push through it, with a great sigh of relief, we struggled on a little further not knowing where the road or the curb side was when directly in front was this mound of snow, it was as high as the bonnet of the car we pushed about half a car length into it then became stuck fast, after about half an hour trying to move, but to no avail, we set out on the long trudge home, an hour later after a warm and hot drink I in my wisdom decided to go back to the car with a shovel and dig it out, no way it ended up with me locking it up leaving the address on the dashboard and dejectedly head back home. Next morning it was towed out with a tractor and deposited on our drive, thanks guys.

It was a long winter and the work load was quite intense and we had just started planning ahead for one of the very first breed of films labelled a blockbuster – yes it was 'Jaws'.

The terrifying motion picture
From the terrifying best seller:

J A W S

It was going to be our Easter attraction and our pre-marketing campaign started in February. On the home front it had been decided that we should try and move house and get into Bury, it soon became apparent that in 1976 buying one's home was out of our league, it just couldn't be done on our income, so the next best thing was to try for a council house even if only to tide us over until the financial situation improved, Easter was soon upon us and 'Jaws' was opening the next Sunday with four performances daily and a Late Show on Fridays. It was going to be a busy few weeks, we were not disappointed, full houses all the way, on Friday's it was decided to stay at the Mother-in-law's overnight as it would be a 2.00 a.m. finish and I had to be back first thing Saturday morning, at least our three year old son would be able to keep to a regular routine, and it would cut out the journey time. We did this for the four-week run that included late shows.

Easter and 'Jaws' now well behind us it was time to renew my efforts in getting us moved into town, I had been previously been told that we were on the housing waiting list, but this could take at least a year, I wrote to my operations manager and asked if the company would put in an official request to support my application, as usual he came up trumps and within a few weeks we had an appointment to see the housing manager and the offer of a house to view, he was a little perplexed to say the least at our request to wait a while and see if anything became available in the area we wanted to be in, and not just take this, for the sake of, but would if we had to. Another three weeks passed and then it happened, another offer, just what we wanted and in the right area, the deal was done and the move date would be the 4th June 1976.

Back at the cinema business was just mediocre to say the least, it always seemed the few 'good' films that came out went directly to the Odeon, these were the times when the few major film distributors were split between Rank / ABC-EMI circuits which in turn meant that towns such as this that had an Odeon in direct competition we couldn't play their films until much later when they came on stream as second runs. So during these lean years we often turned our smaller screen over to show some very seedy titles. 'Emmanuelle', 'Naughty Nuns', 'Sex Odyssey', 'Young Lady Chatterley', the list was endless, but they cost very little to hire and paid the bills.

If we could only get the projection staffing in some kind of order life would be much easier but there seemed to be no interested ones around, the desperately low pay structure didn't help our plight, Bill was still with me as the king pin, but wanted more freedom to do his own thing, I could sense the feeling it was only a matter of time before he went his own way, as is often the case when young lads start courting or get other interests and no longer want to be tied up evenings and weekends, we was now on our second projectionists in just a few short months, and certainly no further forward it was almost replacing like for like, oh well let's get moved into town and settled in then I could concentrate on this problem.

It was almost June (moving Day) the company had arranged a relief manager to cover my week's holiday, and my dad was coming over to help us move, the week prior to the move was the usual boxing and packaging but the weather had suddenly turned so hot, and seemed to be intensifying each day, right on cue my relief Glen arrived and he turned out to be a really nice guy, that made everything much easier and I took my leave without any reservations.

So this was it 'moving day'. Into Bury early and pick up the hire van, 10.00 a.m. and it was already 80 degrees, but we got the job done, it took three journeys and by the early evening we were all pretty shattered, but here we were in our new abode, on what turned out to be the hottest day for fifty years, we didn't need reminding.

Over the next week I saw quite a lot of my relief, Glen, as I had billeted him with my mother in law for the duration, and that to my surprise turned out very well, so we all became very friendly and a world away of my previous encounters with relief personnel.

By the end of my break, our new house was all ship shape and I returned to work feeling much more secure in that my home life was looking very settled and I was on the doorstep with work, so to speak.

But just a few weeks later Bill handed me his written notice it was expected, nothing wrong, he just wanted a change of direction, so back to the drawing board.

CHAPTER 22

During the week would you believe young Eddy came in to ask if we had any work going as he was between jobs, so the team was complete again, after a settling in period the projection room seemed to have settled down nicely and I could concentrate on the downstairs problems, I had recently taken on two young students for a few shifts per week to bolster the staffing and help cope with the new influx of business, but this hadn't gone down very well with the few older staff members, who had ruled the roost during the years before my promotion, and just wanted to keep the status quo.

They could make life very difficult every time I wanted to implement some new ideas. It didn't matter what you did, you could only be as good as the team around you, I was bemoaning this to my regional manager on one of his visits, he picked up on my frustrations and said that's it then we will bring in the retirement policy clause, three of the main ring leaders were well into their seventies and just used the job as an escape from living on their own, the others would most likely just fall into place after the event. The deed was done the onus was taken from me and was actioned as a company streamline decision. I must say I was dreading them receiving their letters and retirement dates, but it all went off very smoothly and we all had a little staff get together to mark the end of an era.

Over the next few weeks my Regional Manager 'Bunny' Morris was absolutely correct, the remaining experienced staff completely changed their attitude with regards to the task ahead, and we now had four young students doing part time shifts and bringing in fresh ideas and enthusiasm, we never looked back.

The only worry I had was that Eddy was often poorly, and looked it on many occasions, then one day he informed me that he had been diagnosed with Leukaemia and would have to start having treatment, but didn't want to give up work, I made him a promise that I would do everything possible and even cover for him during his treatment visits, this went on for three months and I could see him getting more and more poorly, then he was admitted to Addenbrooke's Hospital in Cambridge which was just a bit too far away for a quick visit as the workload had intensified again, then came that dreaded phone call, Eddy had succumbed to this terrible illness, and I suddenly felt so guilty that I had not visited him in hospital, and now he was gone. A few tears were shed when I broke the news at home later that night.

Here we go again, try and find a projectionist. This time we had a favourable applicant, Derek he lived locally, and had several years' experience in London cinemas before moving to Bury St Edmunds. All that was several years ago, but he still had the knowledge and was to become our chief. He settled in quickly and soon began to make a contribution to the smooth running of the operation.

We had some laughs at the different experiments we tried out such as the time we had this popular film opening 'Back To The Wilderness' it was to have a major television promotion, thinking back to the time of 'When The North Wind Blows' and the problems we had trying to accommodate all those people we came up with this idea to run the same film through both projectors simultaneously, we rigged up a roller system so as to allow the film to travel across from one projector to another, then the two of us would both start each projector in unison and away they both went, oh dear one projector was running slightly faster than the other and the loop of film that went across the room was getting tighter, after about half an hour we had to stop or else the film would have snapped, back to the drawing board, this time we reversed the procedure and fed the film through the fastest projector, this way the loop would grow instead of shrink, so off we went again, after about an hour the loop was touching the floors we devised a holding unit for the film to gather in, it all seemed to work a treat, and over the next week we had several morning training sessions.

Then came the real thing, we had a Saturday morning show followed by a lunchtime matinee, we decided to see how many came in the morning before making a decision it turned out it was just about one screen full so we only used the one projector, the afternoon matinee was going to be it, the queue started forming early, so the plan was to get both projectors set up just like we had practised then when it became time to start I would run up to the projection room and we could do a dual start, would you believe that by start time screen one was just about full so the plan was to get them started then rush down and start filling screen two, off I went we started both projectors, dream start, nice one should run straight through now I'll get the rest of the people in whilst the adverts are running, OK all yours now, wait a minute where's the loop gone it's tightening up on us, going to snap in minute, what's gone wrong it worked every time during testing.

Between adverts we had to do a quick shutdown of the screen one projector to allow the loop to form again and avert a film break, still puzzling over what we had done wrong, then the penny dropped, of course one projector had already run a show and was warmed through and free running the other was still cold and tight, we abandoned the screen two show and at the end of the adverts shut down and moved everything onto the one projector, we never tried that experiment again, my projectionist was quite traumatised with it all, but it would have worked, never mind.

Over the next few months' work had panned out nicely and everything seemed to be running smooth, business was now buoyant, one of my cashiers Joan had been upgraded to become full time and do managerial relief duties, in no time at all she was to become known as my assistant. It was during this tranquil period we decided to have a family holiday, this time in Scotland, something well away and completely different, and we were all so looking forward to it, I had requested and got Glen the relief manager that covered my moving week two years earlier to work alongside Joan for my two-week vacation. After what seemed like an eternity planning routes and timings we were off, Inverness here we come.

CHAPTER 23

I spent the Friday morning picking up the hire car, a Ford Cortina Estate and packing our cases, etc., in the rear, we would be taking Stuart out of school at lunchtime, then setting off. By eleven o'clock the sky just got blacker and by our one o'clock set off time the rain was pouring down, unfazed, off we set heading for the A1 and the North and what an horrendous drive it was with the roads awash, five hours later the skies started to brighten and the rain stopped just in time to take in 'Scots Corner', as we were now veering off the A1 and taking a more scenic route we would drive for another hour or so then find a nice spot to have a brew up and a sandwich.

After pulling off the main road into a secluded layby overlooking a North Yorkshire viewpoint I started setting up the mobile picnic table and my treasured purchase from a recent car boot sale a brass primus stove with Arabic print etched on it, the film influence once again as it was my brew up session in 'The Khyber Pass'. The bubble soon burst as I realised that no mugs and cups had been packed and that eagerly awaited brew up would not be forthcoming, I embarrassingly re packed and set off not saying a word, after just a few miles I spotted a large house with a Bed & Breakfast sign and a thought flashed into being, would they sell me a couple of mugs? In no time at all a ring at the door and after the initial astonishment of me blurting out my dilemma the lady produced three glass mugs, a pound each please! Worth every penny to me as I triumphantly returned to the car and promised that long awaited cuppa at the next layby.

The plan was to stop at Jedburgh for a short break then move onto Edinburgh, park up somewhere near the forth bridge and set off again in daylight after a sleep in the car, best laid plans. By four o'clock it was so cold sleep was not an option so it was decided to move on so as to warm the car up, so my big moment of driving across the forth road bridge was done in darkness, never mind it was all nice and warm inside now and the other three had dozed off so I just steadily coasted onwards, it was an amazing experience driving along watching the dawn break over the mountains and saying after rounding every corner "look at that" only to get a few grunts of approval. After another hour or so I decided to stop and make an early morning cuppa, it seemed that every time we stopped a new experience was had.

This time a babbling brook running close by and the early morning mist lifting from the ground, sheep bleating in the distance and the bird sounds made that moment a special brew.

It was eight o'clock in the morning when we drove into Inverness the sun had come out and our first view of the city was the castle gleaming in the early morning sunlight, then turning the corner into the main street there across the road this banner 'ANDY STEWART SHOW OF THE NORTH' Gerry had been an avid fan of his for well over twenty years and here he was, on that very same day tickets were booked at the Eden Theatre that was her holiday made, but it was a good show and she met her star afterwards, and he recalled her letters and gifts to him and his family, impressed or what: little did I know then that we would see his show again two years later at the same theatre when we took my mum and dad with us on a return visit. Then a few years after that we were invited to his home in Banchory and what a momentous occasion that turned out to be with Gerry and Andy Stewart performing a song and dance routine in his living room and then being presented with one of Andy's much loved possessions from the late great Harry Lauder walking stick collection, a holly root cane that belonged to his wife. It now has pride of place in our glass cabinet.

Over ten years we visited Scotland five times, that's how much of an impact this first visit had on all of us, one of these days we shall go back again.

Geraldine with the walking stick given to her by the late Andy Stewart

Every day was a new adventure and we never stayed still for a moment we planned a different place to visit and explore each day, Nairn a seaside of sorts just past Fort William, they had a small cinema unit showing Kirk Douglas in 'Cactus Jack'. I wanted to go in for a look round, but got shouted down; next day we would visit a small place Killin where they were holding a miniature version of the Highland games, and what a lovely time we had listening to the Black Watch pipe band, and great entertainment. Once back at base I would set the agenda for the next day. This time it would be a drive along the Loch Ness road, stopping at Fort Augustus then onto Spean bridge a WWII war memorial, next stop would be Fort William and Glen Nevis, once there a good look at 'Ben'.

The next day we would take a completely different direction

And go up country to Skye, so much to see and take in but alas the week soon came to an end and it was time to make that long journey home, but what a week we had experienced and we were already planning a return visit. Once back home I still had four days before returning to work so took full advantage of the lovely weather and did plenty of local sightseeing.

CHAPTER 24

Back to work, it's surprising just how much piles up and waits for you to get back, the biggest blow was that my chief projectionist had decided to move on, domestic problems had finally swayed him, so here we go again, the usual misfits came from the press adverts, then out of the blue Frank the chief from the Odeon, or Focus as it was then after a sell out to the Brent Walker Group.

He called in to see how we were coping and volunteered to do some part time hours to help us out if we wanted, as the Focus was going on to part time opening. Frank being on board was like a breath of fresh air; we shared a common goal to keep improving what we had to work with and over the next two years challenged the company in our efforts to improve our lot.

Screen One was our first mission we still had this awful periscope system that was getting worse with age we considered the structure to be unstable and flagged it up to the company, which in all fairness sent their building surveyor down to conduct a survey the long and short of it he agreed, it was unsound but not dangerous. Plans were drawn up to build a separate projection room on the side of the building so as to allow 'direct projection' and then remove the lower section of the periscope shaft. So started the waiting game, weeks turned into months and still no movement and no answers as to when, then quite by accident I overheard a conversation during one of the area manager's rare visits that the job had been shelved. I consoled Frank's disappointment when telling him what I had overheard by saying 'leave it with me'.

The next day I was speaking to the Environmental Health Officer, someone I had got to know over the years when submitting our annual licencing application. I had a site meeting and showed him our problem, and bemoaned the fact nothing was going to be done about it, whoops within two days the company had notification that if the original recommendations had not been implemented a closure order would be put on that screen, after that things began to move a builder had been engaged and steel work ordered and the construction of our new projection room commenced.

We watched its progress on a daily basis Frank was in his element when it became time to start fitting in conduit power lines and switchgear ready for the positioning of the projector. After a few weeks a switch over date was made that would entail an overnight work schedule where after the last show we would have to dismantle the projector and all ancillary equipment, move it down to the new projection room and start the process of rebuilding and wiring ready for pre-show tests, to help us with the more intricate elements of the job a free-lance projection engineer was also going to be with us that night.

What a relief, whilst this was happening the builders would be erecting a tower and removing the mirrors and periscope housing that projected from the ceiling it was around eight o'clock in the morning and we were ready for some screen tests, but the builders were re-fixing the hole in the ceiling where the shaft had come through. Upon going down to find out how long the tower would be in place the cinema was a total disaster zone, bits of plasterboard and ceiling tiles and of course years of dust had scattered everywhere, oh my, why didn't they sheet it up: after a few hectic phone calls a team of staff would be in to start cleaning, we eventually started the testing and lining up and by two o'clock the cinema was ready for the opening, all spic and span and with a picture quality like we had never seen before.

CHAPTER 25

It was now 1984 and the poor old Focus had finally succumbed to be demolished to make way for a new shopping complex. The good thing for us was that Frank would become our permanent chief projectionist and now we could really get out teeth into the improvements we wanted to achieve.

Whilst the Focus lay in darkness waiting for the demolition to start and Frank still had some keys we made several visits to see what was left after the strip out that could be useful to our plans, we were not disappointed and could often be seen struggling the short distance between cinemas with various strange objects, even the curtain tracks, and we carefully removed the screen, it was our intention to make ourselves two screens out of it to cover the painted board we had to use.

For the next few months every minute we had was taken up with cutting down pieces of equipment to fit our own requirements, we made curtain tracks for each screen, and cut the large perlux screen into two and carefully put eyeholes all round as a cinema screen is stretched across a frame just like a drum skin, pulled tight so no creases would show and as we didn't have any framework we screwed wooden batons round the old boarded area and screwed hooks and eyes all round at six inch gaps, then laced our newly made piece of screen onto the hooks, with this done it was then time to mask out the picture area with black cloth which would cover all the eye holes and hooks, and give a nice sharp edge to the projected image, and once we tried out a picture test it was immediately obvious just what an improvement a proper screen made, the picture was so much more reflective, with a good sharp focus. With those improvements stirring us on we wanted to move on to the next stage and have some screen curtains, we had enough different materials from various places all stashed away. Now Frank's wife, Josie, was a seamstress and I will never know how he coerced her into sewing this giant piece of fibre into a festoon curtain. That meant seams and webbing to make the loops at every three foot interval so a draw wire could pass through the eyes which meant the curtain could raise evenly. Whilst she was performing this miracle we were setting up a pulley system that would run on a wire cable to the motor that would lower and raise the curtain, at the same time we would be laying cables from the projection room control panel to the back of the screen, all pieces of equipment we had earlier salvaged from the old Focus. This labour of love went on for several weeks until that final fitting day and how chuffed we were at the end result, it gave a complete new look to our presentation, and most of our regular customers gave the commendations. With this flush of success, we went on to do the other one. We knew what to do now, but this time we would have drawing curtains, we had the tracking, they just needed adapting, so away we went again.

I don't think the company really knew how to respond to this sudden burst of energy and enthusiasm, but took great delight in the increase in business since the press coverage of our endeavours. Two months later the Studio cinema in Chorley was closing and we put out feelers as to what condition the seats were in, it came back that they were ours if we wanted to go up there and collect them, yes please.

We hired a van and set off on the appointed day, eventually arriving at lunchtime. After a look round this now closed down cinema one shock became apparent all the seats were still in situ, it was not going to be a case of load up and get away; luckily we had the trusty toolbox with us. It was mid evening by the time we had 200 seats dismantled and loaded on to the van.

Hasty goodbyes and on our way, it was past midnight before we arrived back home, what a day. It wasn't long before we had made inroads in replacing many of our worn out seats in favour of these wedge back green tip ups, with these jobs all done we trundled along for another six months, then suddenly we were informed that the company had sold out to Cannon Cinemas and we could expect a visit from their representatives in due course. And that was about it from the Star Group Of Companies, a few goodbye phone calls from various persons and now we waited for our new masters.

CHAPTER 26

August 1985 we had been looking over our shoulders for the past few days when a stranger came in carrying a bag with the Cannon logo on and introduced himself as the regional manager who would be looking after us.

After a guided tour of the premises he went to the office where he proceeded to give me a run down on what to expect, it soon became apparent that there was to be some major changes and Canon were very progressive in their vision of the future for the company. It was not really a surprise as I had been reading up on Cannon in the trade magazines recently the words 'The GO GO Boys' had drawn my attention to read more about their exploits from making some cheap promotional films in Israel and flooding the teenage market with 'Lemon Popsicle' and a splash of TV advertising to give it credence, no matter it worked and set the scene for these two Israelis to buy out the Classic cinemas from Lew Grade and start growing the Cannon empire.

Two days later, notification came through that all Star managers were to attend a meeting at the Regent Hotel in London; the only instruction was 'bring a holdall' with you to carry all the new bookwork back.

10.00 a.m. standing outside the Regent Hotel hoping to come across a familiar face. I had looked in the entrance lobby and noticed a directional sign 'Cannon Cinemas Meeting Room', but didn't really want to walk in on my own, so after a few more minutes of pacing a group of apprehensive faces appeared round the corner, I was no longer alone, after the usual greetings in we went to meet our fate, greeted at the committee room door with an introduction pack, and name badge.

There was about thirty of us that had been taken over with the acquisition of the Star Group Cinemas, as we all took our seats, overshadowed by the head table raised on a platform where all the department heads of cannon were seated, the Managing Director, Mr Barry Jenkins, introduced himself and gave a short insight into the origins of Cannon Cinemas then introduced the others at the top table. This intro did break the ice and you could feel the tension subside. Each department head gave in turn a presentation on their particular role and handed out all the new bookwork we would be taking back with us for immediate implementation, some more detailed than others. This went on for the next three hours and most heads were throbbing from all the input that was forthcoming.

The lunch break was a great relief but we would start again in an hour. The afternoon session was more light hearted with all the monetary and legal business being done. The film booking department was next and we were given a run down on the new releases coming our way and the person who would be responsible for programming each cinema, following that came the Marketing department highlighting the company's expectations of us in marketing all these new titles, and woe betide anyone who fell short in the marketing stakes. As the working day came to a close it was time to gather up all these books and ledgers and return to site to spread the word. The initial instruction to bring a holdall was no exaggeration as we nearly all struggled out with more than we ever anticipated, me I stopped off in Oxford street and bought a second bag to share the load what a day this had been, now we had to go back and sell the Cannon ideal to the rest of the staff.

The company head office guys would be coming round to visit each site on an individual basis. The very next week we were informed that the Cannon managers held a yearly convention and this year all the Star managers were invited to join them, it would be a good way of learning what made the Cannon Company tick and get to know other Cannon managers, blimey this was all very different, within the week the details started filtering through, the conference was being held in Majorca, flight and hotel details would be forthcoming, bloody hell I didn't even have a passport and had never flown before, this was going to be one of those adventures. I had three weeks to prepare; the flight was from East Midlands Air Port 8.30 a.m. other Cannon managers would also be on that flight so it was hoped we would meet up en-route. With three days to spare my new passport turned up and I had all things packed that I would need. Work was ticking over nicely, Joan was going to hold the fort for a week, and that visit still hadn't taken place, it wouldn't now until after this convention.

It was day one and time for the off I left home about 1.30 a.m. for the drive to Birmingham airport, not being sure how long I would need but didn't want to be late. By 3.45 a.m. I was all parked up and the place looked deserted it was going to be a long wait, but at least I was here. About seven o'clock things started to happen, staff and customers were milling around, I was on strange ground but taking note of the different flight gates time boards, etc., if I looked at my flight tickets once it must have been a dozen times then suddenly there it was up on the board baggage now being taken, a few people beat me to it as I joined the queue, checked in my case and got a boarding pass which moved me to another waiting area. As the time ticked on towards eight o'clock the waiting area was filling up I was looking over each person wondering 'are you a Cannon manager' most of these people seemed like holiday makers, so as the boarding started I just followed the rest of them and duly stepped onto the plane, it was one of those strange not knowing feelings as I took my seat directly behind the wing and by the porthole, I watched and waited until the door closed and the plane started to taxi whilst we all had a pep talk on safety and survival. By the time this was over we were on the main runway engine noise increasing then it felt like the brakes had just been released and off we went gathering speed while I gripped the arm rest, my stomach suddenly dropped then I realised we had taken off as I watched all below getting smaller and with fascination as the wing changed shape, after a while we levelled out and the remove seat belt light came on, I didn't undo mine, the engine noise was louder than I expected but a constant sound so this was it for the next five hours. A drinks trolley came trundling down the aisle, yay, I think I could handle one of these so there I was at nine o'clock in the morning having a whiskey and soda, breakfast would be served at ten. I found it fascinating looking out at the different cloud formations and sights far below, breakfast came and went and we were well over half way and still no contact with any other Cannon manager, no matter the instructions said there would be a coach to take us to the hotel, all I needed to do was look for that. In no time at all we started descending, ears a popping you could say, but it didn't last long and I concentrated on the outside view, the ground getting closer and the wings changing shape again. Next thing you knew there was a slight lurch then the ground was rushing past; we had landed.

It was during the wait for the baggage arrival that I noticed someone with a Cannon lapel badge so I introduced myself and lo and behold I was not alone anymore. As we left the airport and found the coach with our hotel name on we sat back and waited for the drive into town, this would be my very first experience of being on foreign soil, and I was going to take it all in.

At the hotel reception we were greeted by some familiar faces that I recognised from our very first meeting with Cannon in London, and here they were giving me another name badge and more instructions on which meeting room and the daily agenda, etc. The first few days were quite strained it seemed 'them against us' but after getting to know many of the Cannon managers via the different workshops attitudes started to thaw and by the end of the week I had made some very good friends and new colleagues.

It became very obvious that Cannon considered the Star Group had sold them short once they got chance to inspect the recently purchased premises, and the MD stated that although no final decisions had yet been made there would be several sites that would not be integrated into the Cannon Group. Following the conference it was their intention to visit each Star location on an individual basis before coming to any conclusion. The one condition of the sale of Star Group Cinemas was that NO site visits would be untaken before the completion of the sale, what they didn't realise until after the event was that the Star Cinemas were in a fairly run down state, some worse than others.

With this news still ringing in our ears, the conference week was over and it was time to make the long journey home, where we knew all our staffing teams would be waiting for a full report.

CHAPTER 27

By the time it became our turn for a visit we expected the good thing to be some capital investment into our cinema that was by now looking tired and worn due to the recent onslaught, but on a site visit with our new masters I overheard the Head Honcho Mr Jenkins say to his fellow directors, "Look at this place, let's just close it down and be done with it." What a blow for us as a team that had put our all in to the building, in-house plans were hurriedly formulated, luckily I still had on board the service of the chief projectionist (Frank) from the old Odeon/Focus since its demise. It wasn't too hard as he had started his cinema career off in this very building as the Central, and together we set to with the intention of improving on the modifications we had previously done. We would not be going down without a fight.

Refurbishing our main screen

Job all finished

The new company stood back and watched in amazement as we systematically teamed together and refurbished the cinemas from mostly closed down venue cast-offs; our festoon curtains came from the old ABC in Ipswich when it closed many years ago. During that month we travelled all over getting bits and pieces from as far away as Doncaster for 200 better quality seats and Castleford for another projector. They installed a new heating plant to finish off the works for us. Nothing more was said about closure and that spurred us on to a new level of promoting our cinema and being at the heart of the community. We were a major contribution to the Bury Film Festival and we premiered such films as David Lean's "A Passage To India" and John Boorman's "Hope and Glory". In both instances we were proud and privileged to have Nigel Havers and Ian Bannen to be at the opening of these performances.

Nigel Havers, The toast of the evening.

However, it isn't all fame and stardom when trying to promote a film. Like the time I dressed up as Fievel, the lead character from the animated movie "An American Tail", but it was great fun bringing smiles and laughter to the Bury Carnival crowds

Fun days as Fievel

It was during this period that Dad had been taken ill I don't think anyone at that time really knew just how serious it all was as he had taken to his bed and become a bit of a recluse. We were trying to get home as often as we could and after a discussion with Mother it was decided she should call in the doctor and just not tell him until he was here. The very next day she did just that and within the hour Dad was being transported by ambulance to Peterborough General Hospital. I arranged a day off so as to meet up with most of the family; there was to be a family meeting with the consultant so after we had all in turn visited Dad's bedside it was now time for that meeting. We all sat there full of apprehension whilst being explained to, in the kindest possible way, that he had cancer of the stomach and of the most malignant type. It was inoperable and the very best diagnosis was between two to three months, in the meantime they would perform some surgery and make him as comfortable as possible. We left that room in a state of shock, all of us, we knew it was not that good, but never expected it to be that bad, no one knew what to say to each other, so it was a long silent journey back home to Mum's. Later during the evening we all started to open up and make plans for the future, and how to cope with what lay ahead. Thereafter most of us had to make our way home to our respective parts of the country, but would be in daily contact.

For the next few weeks every off day was spent in going home either as a family or on my own, sometimes direct to the hospital if Mum was already there. Then we were told that Dad's wish had been granted and he would be coming back home. Hasty rearrangements were made to turn the front room into a bedroom. The day he came home I couldn't be there but by all accounts it was very traumatic and brother Alan was a rock to all. It would be five days before I could get off work and go home, a Sunday, a day I shall never forget, the shock of seeing Dad, he had deteriorated so much in those few days I never left that room or his side for the entire day, spending a lot of time massaging his feet and legs, trying to put some life into those ice cold limbs (it's not until a long time after you remember the phrase dying from the feet up). Upon leaving for home I promised I would be back early on Tuesday, my next day off. I rang home twice on Monday for an update; it was not good. Then at seven o'clock Tuesday morning the phone burst into life, it was Mum saying he had gone. After a ring round of other family members I was on the way, that was a drive I just don't remember, but after an hour or so I was walking in and hugging Mum before going in and seeing dad. By lunchtime we were all there, but it was so surreal none of us knew what to say to each other for the first time ever, then the most upsetting event, the undertakers arrived to take our dad away, it was now so final, after that we all took Mum to conclude Dad's business, close bank accounts, etc., visit the undertakers for final arrangements, a few hours later we started to disband and start the journeys home. Before I left town, arrangements were made to pay one last visit to see Dad and say my proper goodbye, I had been told I would feel better after seeing him in a peaceful state, they were wrong, it didn't help and as I kissed him on the forehead I felt worse than ever, but managed to compose myself as I said my goodbyes leaving behind Mum and our youngest brother, Adrian. The next time we would meet up would be the funeral day, my journey home was quite traumatic, my mind was racing through the day's events until I had to pull off the road and just burst into tears. I think the past three months had finally caught up with me, after a short while I gathered myself together and journeyed home to my own loving family.

Funeral Day, we arrived in good time to what seemed an empty cold house, wreaths and flowers laid out in the front hall, a constant arrival of brothers, sisters and relations, the hearse was stopping off at mid-day and we would follow in procession the fourteen miles to Peterborough

Crematorium the final part of the journey, where we met up with Dad's family members from his home town. After the cremation and all the chats with aunts and uncles we had not seen for a long time we then made our way back to Mum's with the few that wanted to join us, later that day my sister Susan agreed to take Adrian back to London with her so he could pursue a banking career in the city, this of course meant that Mum would now be completely alone but she was adamant that he should go with her blessing as it would be the making of him so tomorrow they would on their way. During the evening most of the family members were leaving to travel back to their different destinations and when it became our turn I promised to ring each day for a chat and update, of which we both did and it seemed that she was settling quite nicely, for me I was having grave problems coming to terms with the realisation that Dad was gone; he had been so interested in and supportive of my work and everything we did as a family, and now it was the knowing he was just not there. I threw myself headlong into work just to try and block it out, but the thoughts and visions would not go away. Then one night and I remember this as vividly as if it was only yesterday – me coming down the stairs and sitting on the settee with MY DAD. I even remember asking him questions and him telling me that he would not be able to come back again he was going to a different plane, whatever that meant, I don't remember going back upstairs, Geraldine does, but I do know from that moment on an inner peace came to me and I have never grieved over him since, sad yes! But that's a different feeling.

CHAPTER 28

November 1986 company conference time again and rumours had been running rife as to where it would be held until the day the envelope arrived and what a shock the entire management of the company were travelling to Israel the homeland of the Go Go boys Golan & Globus and they wanted to give us an experience we wouldn't forget, and to top it all they were going to invite three projectionist who had shown outstanding merit to join the party, and our Frank was one of the elite group, it really was their way of saying well done for all the renovation works, Frank was over the moon.

On the appointed day we travelled to Heathrow Airport where we would meet up with at the rest of our delegation for the onward journey on an Ell-Al 747 Jumbo, after what seemed like an eternity of waiting around our flight was called and we were boarding, a few palpitations, but just follow the flow and don't look scared despite all those past airplane films flashing into the mind, it was dark outside so nothing to look at and concentrate on Frank he was a few seats away from me but I could see he was as white as a sheet, his first flight, but a thumbs up sign from us both and we settled back whilst the usual pep talk took place, whilst this was happening the plane was slowly taxying to the runway then with a roar it was up and away so just sit back and enjoy it from now on, the drink trolley will be round soon, a couple of snifters would see me right they did: along with the in-flight meal. I must have had a snooze as the next thing was waking to the sound of the seat belt warning, I was three seats away from a porthole so it was just a dark opening, when suddenly the exterior lit up and made several of us jump, at the same time an announcement came over that we would hit some turbulence during landing as there was a raging storm below, just as the outside lit up again, and again. I managed to deduce that it was the flashing light on the end of the wing reflecting against the cloud base we were passing through, the plane rocked and bumped until suddenly lurching onto terra firma and the realisation we had landed. As the plane came to a standstill you could see the rain lashing down the porthole, seat belts off and get your hand luggage from the overhead cabinets and be ready to exit, came the instruction, as we left the plane by way of the telescopic corridor you could hear the rain and actually feel the wind buffeting it. I thought Israel was dry and warm, but as we walked to the luggage collection area you could see out of the windows across the airport, palm trees actually bent over by the wind, after another eternity of a wait some luggage started to appear, once cleared there would be coaches to transport us to the hotel, it was a dark wet and windy drive to the Hilton in Tel Aviv three coachloads off that flight all laden with luggage, it was quite chaotic for a while checking in and getting the week's itinerary. Frank and myself were sharing a room. After unpacking and having a well-earned cuppa we sat and studied the week's schedule, not too many meeting, trips out most days in fact it was more a mini holiday culminating on the last day with the Gala dinner and award ceremony. The next morning it was breakfast then a general meeting in the hotel conference room a light lunch and coaches for a sightseeing trip to Jerusalem. In fact the first three days was very much the same pattern with tours of Bethlehem and the wailing wall, the third day was a trip to the cannon film studios some of it was still under construction but films were being shot there and sets were busily being built. The entrance was a castle frontage all propped up with scaffolding and a shell of a carriage resting on some tin drums, a pair of steps for the actors to climb in and two long handles for the crew to give it a rocking motion, to me it was all so fascinating, walk into another prop room and there was a massive pile of 'wooden' machine guns; amazing what you can get away with on screen. The director of the studio gave us all a pep talk on what they were going to achieve pointing first this way then that way where the rows of chalet-style accommodation for the actors and crew were under construction. He went on to talk about that in, years to come, film would be transmitted from a central station to individual cinemas, it all sounded a bit futuristic to most of us, but here we are some 26 years later doing just that – live transmissions from around the world beamed over and showing on our screens. That day went past so quickly; the only disappointment was there was no filming taking place.

Another day, another excursion this time across the Judean desert (in an air conditioned coach) to the 'Dead Sea'. In the distance was Jordan, we stopped here for a couple of hours for those who wanted to experience floating in the salt water, then onto the mountain range that included ancient ruins from king Herod's rule. Our Israeli tour guide made the entire journey so interesting. Then back to the hotel in time for a fresh up and evening banquet and a look at tomorrow's agenda, another privileged trip but we would not be told our destination until after we had boarded the coaches at 9 a.m. sharp.

This day started out as a bit of a déjà vu, but once underway and leaving Tel Aviv our tour guide informed us that this was something really special and not usually granted to visiting groups; we had been invited to spend the day at Ramat David Air Force Base this being one of three principal airbases in the Israeli Air Force, located south east of Haifa, it was originally built as a Royal Air Force station in 1942 under the British Mandate when it was known as RAF Ramat David. Instructions were given that this was a fully operational station and on no account should any photography be undertaken, failure to heed this warning and the persons responsible would be deemed as spies, bloody hell where were we heading? After travelling for just over two hours we arrived, at the entrance gates and checkpoint the coach was entered and group photos taken of the passengers on the three coaches after that we proceeded to park up and start the guided tour.

The entire route into the station was made up of all these displays and Air Force memorabilia they must have spent days preparing for us, just who are Golan and Globus that they could have persuaded the Israeli Air Force to turn an operational station to an entertainment for us for the day, and by the looks of it they had pulled out all the stops. By the time we had reached the end of the static displays we were ushered into a function room for refreshments and a talk of how the rest of the day had been planned out for us. There would be some lectures and film shows on the development of the Air Force then we would break for lunch and in the afternoon a special Air Display (just for us) had been prepared, and what a display it was with the climax being the vertical take-off of three fighter jets. Our commentator explained that we were only 2 minutes' flying time from the Lebanese border, if they didn't take off in a vertical position they would be out of their Air Space before reaching altitude, so cover your ears and watch it happen. These three Jets roared down the runway and as they left the ground they shot upwards like three rockets going into orbit, the ground actually shook under the roar of the engines and with ears a popping they were gone. It was certainly a day to remember and the topic of conversation once we arrived back at our hotel for the evening meal.

The final day, our morning was taken up with a business meeting with all the Cannon managers (guests not included) and presentations by the different departments on the updates to company procedures and policies as we moved forward once we were all back in our cinemas. This took until lunch time then it was a free day for any shopping, etc., that would take us up to the Gala Dinner and awards ceremony always the grand finale to these once a year weeks away.

The dinner lived up to all expectations, a real glitzy affair and now the awards, the stage was set, Menahem Golan and Barry Jenkins would be giving out the awards to the lucky participants, we on the floor would be cheering on our colleagues, after what seemed an endless procession of lucky winners in all different categories it then came to the 'Biggy' the company's Manager of the Year award, the entire room waited with baited breath for the announcement. Barry Jenkins stepped up to the microphone and delivered a few words which concluded with, "The winner for this year's prestigious Manager of the Year Honour goes to …" (another long pause whilst he shuffled some papers), "… Mr Pat. Church of Bury St Edmunds …" Well knock me down with a feather, the realisation and shock had set in, I don't remember the walk from our table to the stage amidst all the cheering and clapping, but once all the handshaking was over and I stood there clutching my trophy my first thought was 'I wish Dad could see me now,' but perhaps he was there. Back in the hotel room I rang home to tell them the news, I knew that would set the jungle drums going, and it did. Well off to bed, although I was too excited to sleep, but it was to be a long journey home tomorrow and I couldn't wait to be there.

Manager of The Year 1986 Certificate

Frank and myself had a good flight home, much better than the incoming one and we arrived back in Bury at seven o'clock on the button where we parted company and made our respective ways home. As I walked through our front door the reception was amazing with the house decked up with congratulation messages and everyone wanting to know all the details of my week in Israel. Back at work the next morning it was much the same; everyone, staff and patrons alike, all wanting to pass on their good wishes, those jungle drums had been working overtime.

Again several attempts were made to move me away from my cinema, but even the prestigious site at Oxford held no interest for me. It was difficult to explain to someone just how I felt about my cinema here, there was so much of me invested into it and to move away would be a betrayal to my beliefs.

At a manager's meetings in Birmingham I was taken aside by the managing director with the intention of a final push to get me to change my mind and move me on to bigger things as he kept saying, I stood my ground and I really think he finally understood where I was coming from, and the pressure went away and moving on was never mentioned again.

CHAPTER 29

As in many company boardrooms, overseas deals, and banking mergers affect us all and Cannon was no exception, as the company was swallowed up by the MGM group headed by Alan Ladd Jr. It would run as two separate entities and only certain cinemas that met with pre-ordained criteria would become eligible to be re-branded MGM.

We didn't expect a hope in becoming one of these elite few as they all seemed London-based or large city centre sites, but we got together once again and produced a promotional video promoting the virtues of a small town venue compared with a large city site. And by some quirk of fate it worked.

Maybe the MD felt guilty for doubting us when they took over as Cannon and this was his parting gift before being ousted. So our fortunes changed yet again as we became the smallest MGM Cinema ever, and we took full advantage of it in upgrading the inner fabric of the building, having much needed air conditioning installed and a re-seat.

We did it in style and had the Mayor to officially unveil a plaque in our foyer noting the date and the occasion and all the staff were kitted out in the MGM livery, and feeling very proud of themselves, and why not they deserved it.

The Mayor unveiling our MGM plaque

Geraldine modelling the staffs new MGM livery

Managers looking the part making the lion roar

Happy crew makes a happy cinema

So with such a prestigious name above our front doors, it meant the sky was the limit when it came to marketing, so with the release of Disney's The Lion King we arranged a joint campaign with a local wildlife park and secured our very own lion cub to be on site for the opening day, much to the delight of Gerry and myself.

Making The Lion King a Roaring Success

Another year over and time for one of those company conferences. This year it was to be Jersey, flying from Stansted this time, that's more like it. I met up with a few colleagues at the airport and off we went, our final destination would be The Hotel de Paris.

I always enjoyed these conferences, in fact treated them like a mini holiday, as I think was their intention, meeting new faces that had joined over the past year. The week was taken up with meetings on a daily basis of different divisions of the company where we got to hear of the next year's expectations and changes to implement and we could voice our opinions on the different policies, these meetings would be broken up with trips out to local attractions and film shows, as this hotel had its own independent cinema attached, we had a sneak preview of 'Who Framed Roger Rabbit' at nine o'clock one morning, that was a good fun to start the day, a late show of `DAVE` another film I've seen several times since.

But good things soon come to an end and MGM was just a big Monopoly game, and we were put on the open market, within eighteen months, a sell off to the Virgin Group was announced, but they only wanted the pick of the bunch, and Bury wasn't included so we only spent a few short weeks under the Virgin banner not even long enough for a name change. Then coming in to the rescue was our old MD Mr Barry Jenkins who had had the foresight to buy out the ABC brand name some years earlier and all the left over sites formed the new ABC chain.

So the new ABC circuit was created along with all the regular faces we had got to know over the past few years, in fact from our point of view nothing really changed, just a tightening of the money belt, as without all the key situations the company was not so buoyant as it had been, but the enthusiasm from the heads of departments had been triggered and was clearly feeding through and it was a working pleasure to forge ahead with local initiatives which in turn could only benefit the new ABC company of which we were all part, and having steadily upgraded the inner fabric of the building over the past year using the MGM banner as our bargaining point we had fared better than most.

The next couple of years trundled past, this was also the period that the multiplex phenomenon was at its peak with this style of cinema operation opening up in nearly every city and large town usually as a new build retail and leisure area, these premises were all very glitzy fresh and different offering lots of choices under the one banner with ample parking and eateries on the same site.

The flip side to this was that many of the established town centre sites were now seen as out dated and under invested cinemas of yesteryear. It was a sad time to see so many of these once favourite and cherished places of entertainment being closed for redevelopment, or very quickly falling into disrepair and being boarded up. Unfortunately the new ABC Company fell headlong into this trap as the majority of their sites were of the older city centre stock. It soon became very apparent that ABC were running into financial difficulties in trying to keep some of these very large and expensive to operate sites open whilst watching their dwindling audience move over to the multiplexes.

It was about this time that Bury St Edmunds, after several years of fighting off the inevitable, was about to see the foundations laid for a new multiplex cinema from the American group Cineworld.

Then the scaremongering started "That'll be the end of you." "Your days are now numbered." "You won't compete with them." These remarks were endless and only added to the uncertainty ahead.

This plagued us for a few months when suddenly and without any warning it was announced that ABC Cinemas were going to merge with Odeon Cinemas, oh dear I wasn't expecting that, wonder what the future holds for us now? After a couple of weeks of intensive communications, a date was set for all ABC cinemas to be signed over and become Odeon, the company would be transferred over in its entirety to Odeon and any changes needed would happen after that date. They were unsettling times to say the least, mass redundancies from the Head Office staff was the first move, then a programme of cinema closures both ABC and Odeon ones, "A streamlining operation," is how it was put over.

This phase out of the way then new faces started to appear all the ABC cinemas that survived the streamlining were now going to be branded Odeon and have all new livery, it was a very strange time as their administration and accounting procedures were things we had never experienced before, all very heavily linked to central computers, call centres and suchlike. New IT equipment would be installed straightaway: embrace it and learn was the message from Odeon.

Interior signage

Outside new look

From the very outset of moving over to Odeon and the new higher management attitudes it was made very clear to me that Bury St Edmunds was only kept on as it was the only cinema in the town and surrounding area but once Cineworld opened the multiplex they would close our doors and place a covenant on the lease so that no one could re-open it as a cinema. I understood this to be a deal they had made with Cineworld and something they regularly did between them.

The next six months became increasingly difficult as the entire operation was taken over by IT administration controlled by offices elsewhere and unless you had a degree in computer studies it was impossible to follow what was going on, as there would always be some department overriding the systems you were trying to use, explanations and so called training was in a different language than anything I had previously experienced and the workload became more and more stressful. It was all so alien to us to sit down at the main computer only to find out someone in a London office was controlling its functions and all you could do was sit and watch until it was switched back over for local use not knowing what they had done, when questioned it always came back as an upgrade.

At a manager's meeting in London it was noted just how many of my old ABC colleagues were missing, they had one by one moved on to pastures new a sure sign of how the business was changing. It was also at this meeting we were informed that our ABC area manager had taken redundancy and the Odeon Area Operation's manager would be visiting us all during the next week.

But in spite of the downbeat mood, at this meeting I was presented with a Regional Award for the South East Region in the shape of a glass trophy aptly named ODEON OSCARS so we must have been doing something right.

Quarter 1 Regional Winner South East, Bury St Edmunds

Back at base it was difficult, to say the least, putting a smile on and encouraging the staff to remain focused on a positive future, even more so after that fateful visit from the Odeon Operation's manager. We just didn't hit it off, as you do with some people, he was so condescending to say the least and found fault at every different level with our cinemas, staff and administration policies, all the things that were dear to my heart and had kept us in good order for many years past. The meet ended with him handing over a budget sheet that was just not viable or achievable to a cinema of our size and capacity, after a heated argument on the subject it was made clear that this is what was expected and if it couldn't be fulfilled the company wouldn't wait for the multiplex to open and would close the cinema early, so you just get on with it and make it happen.

Over the next few weeks I made contact with Mr Trevor Wicks someone I knew from his coming over to Cannon from ABC. He was a man I respected from previous encounters at meetings and his social visits to my cinema mainly because of his great enthusiasm for the business.

By now he had managed to branch out on his own and acquire some small independent cinemas which became known as Hollywood Cinemas. Now two of these were leased from the same landlord as these premises so that was a good starting point, a dialogue between us developed intensively and it now looked as if there could be life after Odeon as he was sure that a closure covenant could not be enforced.

Whilst our plans for the future were being formulated different departments from the Odeon were still talking of redundancies and closure plans, this didn't seem quite so unsettling now. Then came that fateful morning when I turned up for work and there waiting for me was the Area Operation's manager, and two others, it transpired that some irregularities had shown up in the stock accounting procedures on their IT systems and I needed to explain them – what? After plugging lap tops, etc., into the office IT system and bringing up screen after screen of figures, three people all talking together, 'Look at this,' 'What do these figures mean?' 'Who entered this?' my mind was a complete blur I really didn't know what they were talking about, this went on for a few hours going over all the figure work for the past six months.

I never did find anything untoward, and my suggestion that could they have been entered incorrectly was dismissed straight away.

By early afternoon a pre-arranged plan was put into operation and I was formally told they considered I had either entered false figures in the stock accounting system or allowed with my knowledge someone else to falsify the accounts, therefore I was to be suspended from work whilst a formal investigation could be carried out, would I please relinquish my keys and collect any personal belongings then I would be escorted off the premises at which time I was not to speak to any other member of staff and would be notified by letter when to come in for another meeting. A very shell-shocked manager was led from the building. What had just happened? Where had the job gone that I had always loved so much and worked my heart out for over so many years? I needed to get home and clear my head and formulate plans, I wasn't going down without a fight.

The next day I thought I'd better make contact with Trevor of Hollywood as we were both getting excited at the possibility of 'life after Odeon'. As I was giving him a rundown on what had transpired and the fact I was now on a suspension he out of the blue said, "That's interesting," a very similar thing happened to the Odeon manager here at Norwich a few years ago, he just took early retirement rather than cope with the strain of it. I bet you anything you like they want you out before they close it and have to make you redundant, how long have you been there 38 years is it? Yep that will be it! Although I inwardly felt a lot better after that conversation it didn't stop the feeling of despair that had entered my soul.

After a few days going over and making notes of everything that involved accounting procedures I received the letter inviting me to a meeting in my office in two days' time. What a very strange hour that turned out to be, from the onset the staff had been instructed not to speak, although I could sense they wanted to, upon being taken down to my office which had taken on the appearance of a 'kangaroo court', the reasons for my suspension were gone through in detail then I was given the opportunity to put over any points of my own, which I duly did in the form of written details, the meeting concluded with them agreeing to go through my notes and investigate anything new, another meeting would be arranged for in about a week, at which time a decision would be made on my future.

I left with very little confidence of getting a fair hearing and decided to make contact with BECTU, the Entertainment Industry Union. I was a lapsed member from years past, but felt I needed them behind me more than ever. I sent them a very long missive outlining everything that had transpired and a renewal for my membership. When the reply came back, knock me down with a feather, it was from the very first person I met from Cannon Cinemas the then area manager a person I liked instantly and always had respect for. I had heard he had gone to work with BECTU, small world, a meeting was set up for two days' time when after reminiscing over old times and people long past, we did get down to business it was like a breath of fresh air, he had sat in many of these type meetings before and knew the Odeon people who would be present, we just had to wait now for them to set the date and time then we would attend together, and state our case. I suddenly had a spring in my step and didn't feel alone and despondent any more.

The day of reckoning, the meeting had been set for 11 a.m. on a Tuesday Morning their letter stated that I should have a representative with me and they had appointed someone to 'support' me. I wrote back and told them I was to be represented by BECTU and must decline their offer of support. At eleven o'clock on the dot we presented ourselves to that meeting; some new faces I didn't know had been drafted in and the process started all over again. After 45 minutes' questions and answers with most of the questions coming from my BECTU man we were asked to adjourn so they could deliberate on their next course of action. We left that meeting feeling quietly confident and waited for the recall, with 'plan B' at the ready should it be needed, after what seemed like an age we were asked back in and given the verdict. It was that although there were some figure work errors documented on the system they could not ascertain these had been done deliberately to conceal any wrong doings, in light of this they would leave it on file for six months and after that date it would be completely dismissed from file, I could return to work with immediate effect. It was arranged that I was to meet the very next day with the regional manager who just a few weeks earlier had escorted me off the building, I knew that was going to be a tetchy meeting, but I was ready for anything now and was there waiting for him to arrive which he duly did. After a very cautious start and a cordial chat regarding past events, and that we both held no ill feelings to each other personally, he handed over my working keys and departed so as I could get settled back into routine once again. As always in troubled times my staff rallied round with so much support I felt so proud of them and vowed we wouldn't let any company put us down again.

Whilst this fragile reunion was going on the company was making preparations to close the site down and make the staff redundant. Little did they know that behind the scenes talks were going on with the landlord and Hollywood Cinemas' Mr Trevor Wicks for the continuance of the business under the 'Hollywood' banner.

Friday 9th November 2005, the very last trading day as Odeon Cinemas, all the staff had now been made redundant from today's date, a new start tomorrow.

CHAPTER 30

Friday 10th November 2005 after an all-night work-in removing any Odeon signage and replacing it with The Hollywood Film Theatre we were ready for business as usual under our new identity the very same day Cineworld opened their doors.

A new direction to embrace

With the Christmas and New Year fast approaching business was a lot better than we had feared it would be. But early into the New Year we started to notice the struggle we were having in attracting customers away from a brand new cinema complex that looked modern and vibrant and to the majority age group of regular cinemagoers that was their first choice, it didn't take a magician to notice the box office results were sinking and we were hanging on by the skin of our teeth, we curtailed some of our opening hours to try and reduce the running costs during the expensive heating season of January and February. It obviously helped but only in a small way and Hollywood had to bail us out and prop us up financially on more than one accession, as the next couple of years progressed on the struggle became endless as when business is at a low ebb. New releases were not forthcoming, no repair work and maintenance was getting done, staff are getting disillusioned and decision making with Hollywood was getting more frustrating by the week. This was not something anyone wanted to happen it was just the knock on effect of competing with a new multiplex cinema of eight screens that were monopolising most of the film titles, this was nothing new and in most towns and cities the smaller opposition cinemas had always succumbed and closed down. If only we could get through the first year or two until the novelty wore off, we would stand a chance of survival.

But alas this was not to be the case. Hollywood asked for an on-site business meeting with me to discuss our options, it turned out they could no longer bail us out and had been advised by their financial accountants to close us down with immediate effect. The meeting concluded with the pre-made decision that we would close our doors in one week's time. After informing all my staff of this and spending a sleepless night pondering our future, I decided to make the next phase the way of an open letter to as many independent cinema operators I could come up with offering our business and the unexplored possibilities that could be obtained. Over the next week I did receive several replies all nearly the same explaining that although interested they were not in a position to expand their business at the moment, and wished me luck in my endeavour. Then I received a surprise email from Lyn Goleby the Managing Director of 'Picturehouse Cinemas' and an on-site meeting was arranged for 8.00 a.m. the coming Saturday. I was at the cinema early that morning full of trepidation and excitement, at eight o'clock sharp I spotted this lady looking the building up and down from the other side of the street, I knew straight away that she was the one I was there to meet as I opened the doors to greet her in, I must say from the very first self-introductions I was completely at ease and it was just like giving a friend a tour of the building. After a couple of hours looking over what we had to offer and chatting about business figures and the untapped potential I could foresee that awaited anyone who would take us on, I could sense the interest she had in just what we had achieved so far, but of course nothing is ever straightforward and the business side of the meeting concluded with the stark facts that Picturehouse, although very interested, would not be in a position to go to Hollywood and the Landlord with a deal for at least another three months, in the meantime she would keep in regular contact. With that the meeting was over. What to do! The cinema was now closed for business, could we persuade Hollywood to let us re-open on a lesser scale until such time. After a hurried meeting with the staff we all formulated a plan of action to put before Hollywood this included a slight reduction in pay rates and running the building on a skeleton staff, with this all agreed between ourselves as a way forward a meeting was arranged with Mr Trevor (Hollywood) Wicks at his main cinema and offices in Anglia square Norwich. I had always had great respect for Trevor as he was once our saviour from the bad old Odeon/Cineworld days and we were all quite proud to become the Hollywood Film Theatre it was just a shame that we couldn't move forward in the direction we needed to. Nevertheless the outcome of this meeting was very positive and agreement was reached for us to continue the business and give it another go! And this is just what we did; our closure and re-opening had generated some press interest which in turn helped to upgrade the business figures once we got up and running again. But after a very few months it became obvious that we were just trundling along. The cinemas, now looking tired and worn, needed an infusion of interest and investment if we were going to survive. Behind the scenes I was still in constant communication with Lyn Goleby of Picturehouse Cinemas as it was becoming more and more obvious that we were once again falling behind in getting new film titles on release and our programming times were not conducive to our customer base, this in turn led to some clashes of opinion between us and Hollywood, but on the flip side paved the way for discussions between the three parties involved Hollywood, the Landlord and Picturehouse and after some delicate negotiations a deal was struck for us to become part of the Picturehouse team.

So in February 2010 Picturehouse cinemas came into Bury St Edmunds with the same vision as myself that would challenge the common perception of cinema entertainment and another phase in the history of the Abbeygate Cinema began. Whilst ideas and plans were being put together we had the task of introducing the name 'Picturehouse' and extolling its advantages and vision for the future. During the summer we teamed up with the St Edmunds Bury Festival and arranged an open air screening in the beautiful Abbey Gardens; this event alone brought the name Picturehouse to the forefront and gave us some very favourable press reviews. It was certainly evident that changes were coming.

The outdoor experience

This venture put Picturehouse firmly in the frame

The first stage was a complete refurbishment of the auditoriums along with the state of the art projection technology, including 3D and satellite equipment. Whilst this was taking place we had a six-week closure period which in turn fuelled all manner of imaginations and people were eagerly waiting to see just what had been done to the cinema, and of course what to re name it as the new company wanted to follow its normal pattern of using the town name followed by 'Picturehouse' (Bury Picturehouse). I stood firm and requested we bring the name Abbeygate back into being, but of course unless you were local the name Abbeygate had no significant meaning, as a final resolution to the challenge it was agreed we would have a local referendum and let that decide, as expected All the local populate agreed with my thoughts and the name ABBEYGATE PICTUREHOUSE prevailed.

It was also at this time that we introduced our weekly "Big Scream" presentations which were special performances for new parents and babies and so it became a weekly occurrence to find our foyer ram packed with push chairs and buggies.

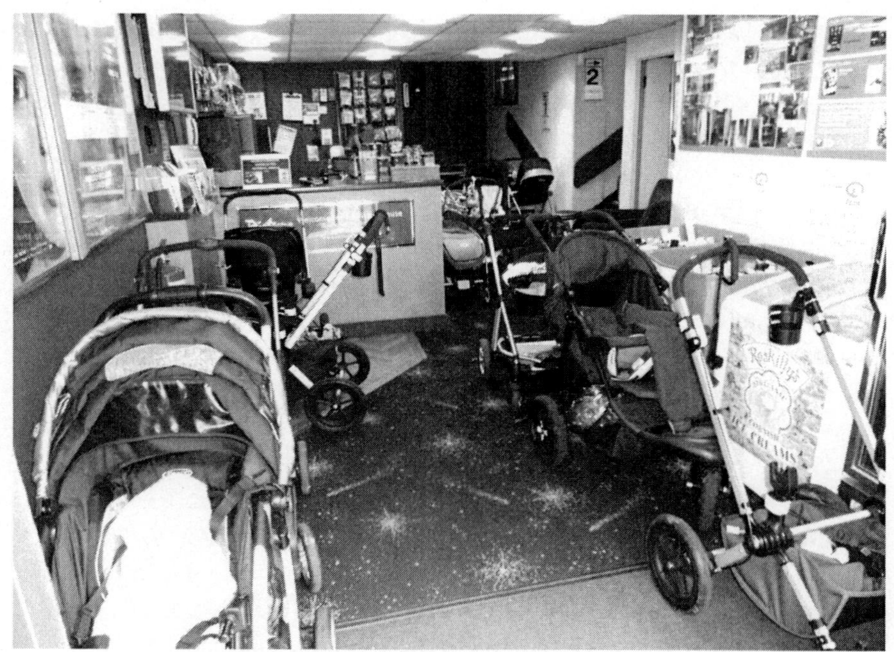

Another Successful Big Scream Morning

The second stage was our new façade and identity: incorporating a new entrance that would move us away from the shared entrance with the attached Bingo Club.

Whilst all these works were going on we were planning and building the third stage (and perhaps the jewel in the crown), this would be the transformation of the empty premises adjoining the cinema, which once complete would comprise a delicatessen-style restaurant and bar.

Going to the pictures would no longer be an in-out venture, as you would be able to combine a relaxing drink or a sociable bite to eat with a good movie.

Our patrons certainly loved the transformation and the local press backed our every move and our business steadily grew. But after all this work and effort we still had stormy waters ahead which were way beyond our control. It appeared that Picturehouse backers dried up and pulled out overnight, leaving them high and dry, so to speak. And would you believe, it was Cineworld that stepped in and bailed them out. It seemed they had been looking closely at this arm of the business and the steady growth over a short few years, but as it was far removed from their own type of operation, to buy into a well-established arts cinema group seemed an ideal solution. Unfortunately for Picturehouse the Cineworld finance package enabled them to take control of Picturehouse by running it as a separate company alongside their own multiplex circuit with the promise that 'nothing would change'. Yeah, sure, I've heard all that before.

After only a few short months the monopolies commission picked up on this and decreed that Cineworld would have the complete monopoly in certain towns and counties, to help control this they decided that at least three sites must be sold off or closed. Aberdeen, Bury & Cambridge. Now this was something that none of us could have foreseen and that air of uncertainty reared its ugly head again. As Aberdeen was leased from the local council this was going to revert back to their control and continue its Art House presence in the city. Cambridge and Bury St Edmunds were going to be sold off as a package deal' this would make the offer very attractive to potential buyers, so let the sale begin. Over the next few months several potential buyers came to view what we had to offer: Some just to nose around, others who wanted to stamp their brand of operation into Bury which was a complete contrast to what we had achieved with Picturehouse and I made this very clear at my weekly meetings with them.

Then it was suddenly announced that Cineworld were moving the goalposts and keeping the Arts Cinema Cambridge and selling off their multiplex complex, that meant we would become a stand-alone site, and would sink or swim on our own merits. Once this news reached all the potential buyers they started dropping out one by one, it seemed Cambridge was the carrot and they thought Bury was just not big enough to go it alone … their loss … Waiting in the background during these negotiation's was a Mr Tony Jones, this was the man who with the current MD Lyn Goleby co-founded Picturehouse Cinemas some 25 years earlier, although he dropped out of the Picturehouse scene some years earlier to concentrate on running Arts Film Festivals up and down the country, he had complete control of the Cambridge annual film festival.

This then set the scene for him to be the front-runner in the Abbeygate sell off stakes, and with the support of Lyn Goleby took control of the Abbeygate Picturehouse on 6th June 2015.

Overnight our fortunes changed yet again. And with this new lease of life we would now be able to offer live transmissions of world class productions from the New York Metropolitan Opera and the National theatre vis satellite direct to our screens. In addition to this we could now introduce our loyal fan base to live broadcasts of the Bolshoi Ballet from Moscow and the Opera De Paris.

With many of the support systems being turned off at midnight that day it really was going to be a sink or swim operation until we got on our feet. Luckily for us we have such a loyal and understanding customer base and they supported us unreservedly whilst the difficult transition was taking place. Cineworld, who now controlled Picturehouse, started to close off the IT systems that we had been buying into on a customer client basis. A month's notice was given that the web site and box office system would be discontinued.

A local Cambridge company was commissioned to create a tailored system for us so as to take over our existing systems. Just this one area created so many problems with memberships, advance booking tracking, our live transmission events and many more IT functions.

It was during this period I, in agreement with the new owners, decided to step back from the control of this new concept of everything computerised, this area of the business had been increasingly causing me so much stress over the past year, it was obvious something had to give, so after consultation with our new owners a deal was struck that I would hand the reins over to my deputy, Jonathan, who was well into this new innovation and I would concentrate on the more public relations and live events, also on the maintenance and upkeep of the inner fabric of the building.

I have to admit that although I was filled with in trepidation as to how

I would feel about stepping back, I see now that I need not have worried. It has settled nicely and my new role has made little difference except relieving me from some of the IT stress that was making me unwell.

About three months into this new process we were informed the Bingo Hall that shares the property with us was closing its doors.

With this being the same landlord we had the first option of taking on the vacant premises and converting it back into a cinema unit, something I have been waiting in the wings for years to happen.

But were we in a position to take it on right now? I needed to put my convincing hat on again and talk to the money men, headed by Mr Tony Jones, although this had come a little early for us, it was now or never.

I felt quite confident that a deal would be struck and an expansion of the Abbeygate Cinema would happen.

Since these events, I have been closely involved in drawing up plans for a new screen and entrance to be added to the premises. Just recently it has just been announced that Tony Jones is now stepping down as Managing Director of the Abbeygate Cinema and is handing the mantle over to a Mr Alastair Oatey – a high ranking person in the Ex-Picturehouse cinemas – who will take control with immediate effect along with Mr Tony Jones who will be a silent member of the new board. The development of the building has now been revitalised and planners and architects are currently working on the next phase.

So if history is anything to go by, we ain't finished yet.

As I complete my 50th year at the Abbeygate it is my one ambition to see this regeneration of the building come to fruition and to be a small part of its success.